THE SCIENCE OF BOYS

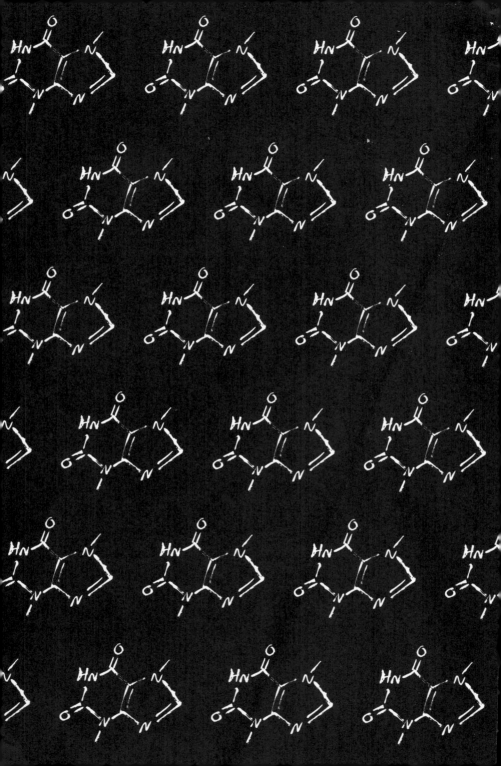

Emily Seo

THE SCIENCE OF BOYS

illustrated by **Gracey Zhang**

TRADEWIND BOOKS
Vancouver · London

For Dad, chemist and storyteller—ES

To the kinetic energy of youth and adolescence—GZ

The publisher wishes to thank Aidan Parker
for his editorial assistance.

Contents

CHEMICAL REACTION

The rearrangement of atoms in a molecule to produce a new molecule.

A, B, C, D . . . same letters as school grades, but not as easy to understand. I skimmed through the bra display but didn't see anything remotely close to my size.

Keys jangled from someone coming near, and I ducked under a rack of satiny pyjamas. Peeking out, I saw an old lady inquire about a pair of Spanx and another lady with her teenage daughter. The girl was probably a couple of years older than me, judging from her height and the size of her boobs. I looked down at the two raisins barely visible underneath my shirt.

A woman crouched down. "Excuse me, do you need any help, young lady?" She was petite and had a distinct hour-glass figure cinched under a belt.

"Um . . ." I stepped out and brushed my bangs off my glasses. "I was . . ." My chin dropped to point at my chest.

"I think I know just what you're looking for." She breezed over to a corner with pastel-coloured undergarments and left me anxiously flitting my eyes between the bra display and the floral wallpaper. The girl with her mom gave me a

confused look: *what business do you have looking at the bras?*

After what felt like forever, I pretended to look for some slippers, gradually moving from one rack to another until I reached the door. *I'll just come back with Mom.*

When I came out of the store, the sun was blazing. I took off my jacket and pulled out my strawberry sun hat before walking toward the harbour to meet Olive.

The boardwalk was packed. Everyone looked like they were soaking up the last few rays of sunshine before summer holidays were officially over. The restaurants and cafés were bustling with people, and laughter was in the air. Although the sky was completely clear, I felt a heavy cloud looming over me.

I don't know why I bother coming early. Olive is always late. I needed something to do while I waited, so I bought a slice of cheese-less pizza and wandered around Fisherman's Wharf. Saul, Steveston's resident sea lion, swam nearby the boats with his muzzle straight up in the air, sniffing the fresh catches of the day.

As I reached the end of the dock, my attention was caught by a girl who sat on the edge, reading a book. There was something familiar about her that drew me in. She raked the hair off her face and gazed outward. She reminded me of Mom. Her expression was tainted with the same look of longing. I wanted to go talk to her, but what would I say? *I can't go up to a stranger.*

She stretched her arm up with the book in hand and revealed a cartoon ink splotch on the cover. *I've read that one.* Maybe I could ask her how she's enjoying the story so far. But when I got close to her, I chickened out.

As I turned around, I dropped my pizza. It landed right beside the girl, crust hanging over the edge of the dock. Saul jumped up for it and pushed her with his massive muzzle.

"Eek!" she shrieked, teetering on the ledge . . .

Splash!

Her arms flailed as she spluttered in the water, and my mind blanked. I could hear people in the distance, but nobody was doing anything. Heart hammering, I searched for anything to keep her afloat. I spotted a lifebuoy on a nearby post. I grabbed it and tossed it her way.

Smack.

Oh no. Her head went back in the water. I covered my face with both hands, peeking through my fingers. *Please be okay.*

Her head popped up. She seemed to be fine—she was conscious at least. She swam briskly toward the dock. I offered my hand, but she just glared at me as she pulled herself up. "What are you doing!" she shouted. "Are you trying to drown me?" Her hair was plastered to her face like kelp, but even then she looked pretty.

"I'm so sorry. Is there anything I . . .".

"Where's my book?"

"I think it fell in with you." I bit my lip.

"Ugh, that was from my dad." She flicked her hair upside down and shook it. Suddenly she flipped back up. "Where's my phone?" She patted her pockets then looked out into the water, running up and down the dock.

I wanted to tell her that it had likely sunk—that a phone was much denser than water, even with all its murkiness. But I kept my mouth shut.

"Thanks a lot," she spouted and stomped away.

I stared out at the water and thought about how that could have gone differently. I would have started by introducing myself. "Hi, my name is Emma. Isn't that a great book?" She would have agreed, and we would have talked about our favourite scenes. Then I could have asked her, "Are you new around here? I've never seen you before." She would have replied, "Yes, we just moved to Steveston. My name

is . . ." I'd offer to show her around, and we'd become fast friends.

"Hey, Emma!" I jumped out of my thoughts to see Olive. We clanked our bracelets together.

"How was Europe?" I asked her.

"Unbelievable! We did a movie tour starting with *Sound of the Mountains* in Salzburg and ending with *Adventures on Arthur's Seat* in Edinburgh. Oh and I learned something new that even you would find interesting. The Eiffel Tower is taller in summer than winter."

"Yeah, it increases approximately fifteen centimetres in height due to thermal expansion."

"Of course you knew. Here I thought I was teaching you something for a change. It's so annoying how you know everything," she said with a smirk.

"Well I missed you too." I stuck out my tongue.

"How was your summer?"

"It was okay . . . aren't you hot in that?" I asked, tugging on her black long-sleeve shirt.

"Black is slimming."

"There's no scientific evidence to back up that theory."

She scrunched her lips. "See, you are annoying."

"If it makes you feel any better, research has shown that a black dot is perceived to be smaller than a white dot the same size, so maybe there is something to it." I shrugged. "Why do you care anyway?"

"I know . . . I shouldn't . . ." She gave me a satisfied smile, and we made our way to Gisele's Gelato. As we neared, the sugary smell of freshly made waffle cones swirled into my nose. We walked to the end of the lineup, which curled around the corner.

"So did you hear?" Excitement flared in Olive's eyes. "The *Magical Creatures* movie did so well, they're adapting it into a TV series."

"Really?" My voice rose even though I wasn't as excited as she was.

The line started to move and we turned the corner. A sign in front of Glo read, FREE MAKEUP LESSONS FOR BEGINNERS. I pointed to it. "We should look into that."

She cocked an eyebrow. "Since when have you been into makeup?"

"It's the start of a new school year . . . I just want a fresh look. Studies show that the way we present ourselves impacts our behaviour, attitude and mood, which end up affecting everything from our social connections to job interviews."

"You'll be fine. You're like the smartest person I know."

Then she dropped her voice. "Plus you don't want to become one of *those* people . . ."

"What do you mean?"

"Who only care about clothes and makeup. You don't want to be superficial."

My eyes widened. "Weren't you the one just talking about what you're wearing?"

"Yeah, but that's different. I'm just trying to . . ."

Olive's voice faded into the background when the girl from the dock appeared. She'd changed into a denim dress with a skinny belt. How did she know to put a belt on with that outfit? Why a skinny belt, not a fat one? And her hair, despite being a little wet, was still wavy and shiny. She stopped and looked at the lineup, turning her head from side to side.

"So what do you think?" Olive must have noticed the blank look on my face. "Are you even listening to me?"

"What do you think of asking that girl to stand in line with us?" Now Olive gave me a blank stare.

As I thought about approaching the girl, who could be from a shampoo commercial, two other girls walked up to her. My heart dropped when I saw it was Ivy and Suzy, my nemeses from elementary school.

I stepped back and hid behind a man's belly as if it were the moon in a solar eclipse. "You're starting Minato High? So are we!" I heard Ivy saying in her fake nice-person voice. I poked my head out to see Ivy and Suzy showing off their necklaces.

"We're next," said Olive. I turned my head toward the

counter display filled with all sorts of delectable flavours. As usual I craved chocolate, but since it was chock-full of dairy, I settled for the vanilla made with coconut milk in a waffle cone. Olive ordered two scoops of cookies and cream in a cup.

On the way out, Ivy caught sight of me and pointed to my strawberry sun hat. "Nice bonnet, Emma. Are you five or something?"

Suzy chimed in. "Yeah, nice hat."

The new girl gazed at me, and I felt sweat trickling down my forehead. Without thinking, I blurted out, "Did you know that strawberries are a good source of ascorbic acid, also known as vitamin C?" *Why did I say that?*

Ivy placed a hand beside her lips, pretending to be discreet, and said, "Geek," but loud enough for everyone to hear. She pushed her elbow into me as they walked away. My cone slipped out of my hand, landing gelato-side down on the wooden planks. It started to melt instantaneously.

"Get a life already!" Olive gave them the stink eye.

I wished I could have done the same, but instead I pushed my glasses up and watched as my ice cream turned to milkshake.

"Too bad you can't have some of mine," said Olive, holding up her cup.

"I know." I hated being lactose-intolerant.

Her expression brightened. "Ooh I heard Minato High has a drama club . . . we should totally join."

"Are you kidding?" I gave her a you-should-know-me-better look.

"Fine. What about movie club?"

"I don't know . . . you should join if you really want."

"I want us to do something together."

"What about science club?"

She shot me the same are-you-serious look I had given her. "I just want this year to be our best one yet . . ."

"Same." My thoughts drifted. *I want to feel good about going to school. I don't want to worry about girls who are mean to me. I want to be liked, not be a geek.* Too bad I couldn't come up with a chemical reaction to convert me into a cooler version of myself. Emma 2.0. For a second I imagined it: from geek to chic.

I snapped myself out of it. There was no point—it was never going to happen.

CELL DiFFERENTIATION

A process by which a stem cell changes to a more distinct cell type.

The sun had just set, leaving an afterglow in the sky. Even in the dimness, our house looked a lot different from our neighbours'. Our grass was yellow, the garden was a pile of dirt, and cobwebs stretched along the bench on our front porch.

As soon as I walked inside, the smell of wet cardboard in gravy drifted toward me. Dad was in the living room reading a science journal with a TV dinner beside him. Scattered around were papers, molecular models and some of our homemade tiles from Elementabble, a game Dad and I made up in which words were constructed using symbols of the periodic table of elements.

"Dad, want to play a game?"

"Not now."

"What are you reading about?"

"Stem cells."

I knew that stem cells were special—that they had the ability to become other cell types like bone cells, skins cells

or muscle cells—I just didn't know why. "What determines the cell type they become?"

"There are many factors." His eyes remained glued to his paper. Before, we would have had a discussion about it, but ever since Dad lost his job as lab director, he'd been a bit of a grouch. Even though he'd got a new lab job, he lacked his normal spark.

I went into the kitchen to search the fridge and found nothing but some condiments, wilted vegetables and clearly past-its-due-date food. In the freezer, I reached for the insta-meal behind an assortment of juice concentrates and Mom's frozen high heels. *I should really clean those before she gets back.* I thought for sure she'd be home in time to take me back-to-school shopping. The microwave dinged to signal my meal was ready, but I wasn't hungry anymore. I composted the food and went to my room.

Less than thirteen hours were left before the first day of high school, and I still had no idea what to wear. From everything I'd read, first impressions were crucial. *I have one chance.* I ransacked my drawers yanking out everything in sight: shirts, shorts, skirts and sweaters, jeans, dresses, tank tops and tights. I examined each item before throwing it over my shoulder. *Too tight, too short, too old. Too worn, too warm, too plain . . . argh, this is driving me crazy!* I had nothing except sweat under my armpits and a room filled with the remains of a wardrobe explosion.

Hoping there was something I missed, I crouched down to search under my bed. I found some dirty socks and tiles from Elementabble. The symbols for nitrogen, erbium and dysprosium—N Er Dy—stared me in the eyes. I quickly shuffled the tiles and pushed them back into the corner. That's when I found my princess shirt, my favourite top that Mom bought me last year for back-to-school. I ran my hand back and forth across the flip sequin crown, switching it from gold to silver then from silver to gold. Finally, I pulled it over my head. It still fit and the sequins were the perfect cover for the two bumps on my chest.

The next morning, I put on the princess shirt with a pair of old but stretchy leggings. My experimental plants on the windowsill drooped out of their pots, so I added some water and homemade fertilizer, hoping for the best.

I still wasn't hungry, but I grabbed a chocolate from Dad's stash and let it slowly melt in my mouth. It made me feel a little better . . . until I put on my raggedy shoes, the only pair that fit.

The sky was blue, but my cloud of gloom still hovered over me. It followed me even when I sprinted. At school, I didn't see anyone I knew hanging around outside the main entrance. The few looks I got were the kind that said, "What are you doing here? You don't belong."

Where was Olive? Why did she always have to be late? I twirled the DNA double helix on the bracelet she made me. She gave it to me when I was going through a hard time, telling me I should never feel completely alone because we were like sisters. "We practically share the same DNA," she'd said and clanked my bracelet with the matching one she made for herself.

Intimidated by all these new faces, I looked down to see that the material on top of my right shoe was about to rip. I forced myself to stand tall and keep my chin up, a posture that oozes confidence. It wasn't long before I tripped and fell on the pavement. A dot of blood trickled down my palm, and right away I felt light-headed. *Please don't faint.* I sat on the edge of the sidewalk that dropped off to the parking lot and quickly took out the latest issue of *Science Today and Tomorrow.* As I began to read the first article, I started to feel better . . . but then I sensed judgy eyes and heard snickers around me. I stuffed the journal back in my bag, wishing I had a phone to flick through like everyone else.

I felt a nudge. "Nice shirt, *princess*," Ivy mocked. "Didn't you have that last year?"

"Yeah," Suzy spewed.

I covered my beating chest with my arms, and Ivy's voice heightened. "You're not hiding anything. It's obvious you're flat as a board." She sniggered with Suzy and a few others joined in. My face heated up, but my feet froze to the ground.

Olive rushed toward me. "Don't body shame her."

Ivy sneered back. "Of course you would say that."

Olive pulled me away. "Don't listen to them."

"Aren't you sick and tired of this?"

"Yeah, but who really cares what they think?"

Unfortunately I did. "How do you just let it go?"

"Like I said before, you're the smartest person I know. You chose me as your best friend, so I must be pretty incredible."

If I were so smart, why couldn't I figure out how to be more sure of myself?

The bell rang and we headed to our homerooms. Not recognizing anyone in the class, I took the first empty seat, but the girl next to me said she was saving it for someone else. So I sat in the next open seat, beside a guy who wore wireless earphones, bopping his head. Our homeroom teacher, Ms Grimaldi, looked strict: glasses perched on her pointed nose, arms crossed and a bun as tight as the knot in my stomach. "Put away all devices!" She plucked the earphones off the guy next to me.

I heard him say, "Will do, Godzilla," under his breath.

While she took attendance, I stared at the ground . . . at my shoes. The material had torn and my big toe poked out of the hole.

"Emma Sakamoto."

I raised my arm halfway before sinking lower down in my seat.

Each of us was given a timetable, some forms, an agenda and a lock with a combination. As I studied my schedule, I heard footsteps approaching.

"Sorry I'm late. My name is Poppy Sinclair and I'm new." It was the girl from the dock. She carried a book with an astronaut helmet on the cover.

Ms Grimaldi's eyes lasered across the room at her. "*All* grade eights are new to this school. Not just you."

As Poppy walked down the aisle, a couple of people pointed to the empty seats next to them, even the girl who told me she was saving the seat for someone else. Poppy sat in front of me and pulled out her phone. I was relieved she'd replaced it so easily. Ms Grimaldi shrieked, "Put that away!" Poppy immediately slipped her device into her pocket, jaw clenched. A few more people referred to our teacher as Godzilla, and although she looked nothing like the giant movie monster, the name spread like a viral video.

We were allowed to leave once we had filled out some forms and proved that we could open our locks. I pretended to work on my completed forms while Poppy struggled with her lock. I was about to offer my help, but the guy next to her slid his chair beside her. He was more focused on her face than her lock.

"Go back to your desk, young man." Godzilla tilted her glasses down at the rest of the class. "You must be able to unlock your lock *by yourself!*"

Most of the class had left when Poppy finally flicked open her lock. This was my chance to apologize to her for what happened at the dock. "Um . . . hi, do you remember me?"

She squinted, saying, "You tried to drown me," and marched away.

My stomach felt sick like I'd drunk milk.

Outside, a swarm of people gathered in front of the main entrance. I tried to squeeze myself through the crowd to see what all the commotion was about, but all I felt were elbows pushing me back out. I spotted a bike rack and climbed up it.

A guy spun himself around on one arm with his fluorescent green sneakers twirling in the air like a boomerang before he froze into an upside-down statue. A bunch of people snapped photos with their phones. One of them was Poppy. With one shoulder she dug herself through the crowd, and people shifted over to make space for her. Within seconds she was at the front, talking and laughing with everyone. How did Poppy make a good impression so easily? How did she know how to act or what to say?

It got me thinking . . . popular kids were like stem cells. They had the ability to fit in anywhere. I began imagining everyone as different cell types: sporty people were muscle cells, rule followers were bone cells, those who protected others were skin cells, brainiacs were nerve cells, and the few who were like Poppy were stem cells—they could become any cell type and get along with anyone.

Was the "it" factor something you were born with . . . or was it something you could switch on? I wished for some sort of book explaining all this, like a scientific guide. Maybe I could hang out with her to find out.

I have to find a way to fix Poppy's first impression of me.

BUOYANCY

An upward force that opposes the weight of an object in fluid.

The next morning I found a package the size of a boot box at the bottom of the stairs, along with a few new dust bunnies. From the way it was wrapped and the neat handwriting, I knew exactly who it was from. I quickly ripped it open to find a note.

"Sorry I couldn't be there for back-to-school shopping."

My heart leapt. *New clothes!* I pictured a chic new shirt with sleek leggings and a stylish pair of shoes.

I lifted the flaps of the box to find a tracksuit with pictures of planets and stars, a junior lab coat and a pair of safety goggles. I was confused. It wasn't like Mom to pick these out. Oh I know . . . she knew it would make Dad smile. Then she'd give me my actual clothes in person so she could see the excitement on my face. *That must be it.*

I called Mom to thank her, and her voicemail beeped.

"Hi, Mom, it's me . . . just wanted to thank you for the package . . . anyway, call me back." I put away the science-y clothes and went to school.

As soon as I entered the halls, someone waved and walked toward me with a smile. *Finally, someone new who's friendly.*

I waved back with an equally big grin, but she briskly walked past and greeted the girl behind me. I kept my arm raised and pretended that I was waving to someone else. As soon as I turned the corner, I clenched my lip and dropped my chin. *Great,* the hole in my shoe had grown.

"Seriously, don't you have any other shoes? We could smell your feet from like a mile away," Ivy said in her usual patronizing voice. Suzy pinched her nose and several others laughed at me. I felt like I was getting sand thrown in my face.

Stand up for yourself. Say something . . . anything. I looked around for Olive, but she was nowhere to be seen. As soon as I could move my legs, I ran.

The thing I looked forward to all day was science class.

I went early to sit in the front row, but then hesitated. *Don't want to seem too eager.* I walked to the second-to-back row and pulled out an issue of *Science Today and Tomorrow.* "How to Design a Homemade Boat," I read. The article talked about why something floats or sinks.

A few people started shuffling into the classroom including the breakdancer with the neon green shoes and George—finally someone else I knew from elementary school. Like me, he hadn't developed much over the summer. He was still short and skinny and sported an oversized shirt, trying to make himself look bigger than he was. But I didn't blame him. In one of those studies that talk about the importance of appearance relative to success, there was a whole paragraph about how CEOs of the biggest companies appear taller than average. George sat next to me and asked me about my summer. "What did you get up to? I barely saw you."

"I was around," I answered.

"Were you out exploring or doing your usual experiments?"

"Something like that . . ."

"I'm psyched we're in the same science class. Hope some of your brain power rubs off on me."

I grinned, until Ivy and Suzy strolled in. They gave friendly waves to a couple of people. I avoided eye contact with them but heard Ivy compliment a girl about her headband. As they neared the back row, she whispered to Suzy, "Makes her forehead look huge." They giggled and sat directly behind me. I braced myself for a snide comment.

Then Poppy walked in, and the breakdancer, along with a few others, watched as she read something on her phone.

"Hey," Ivy hollered. "Come sit with us."

Poppy walked toward them, right past me. I wanted her to see through Ivy and Suzy—to see how mean they could be—but Ivy's voice was sweeter than ever. "Love your shirt."

Suzy agreed. "So cute."

Why couldn't they be that nice to me?

A second after the bell rang, Olive came in wearing a *Magical Creatures* T-shirt. She sat in the empty seat next to George and reached around him to clink her bracelet with mine.

"Geek squad," Ivy coughed abruptly.

Almost as abruptly, our teacher stumbled into class with a misbuttoned lab coat and crooked safety goggles. "Good afternoon, class. My name is Mr Timberlac." He raised both his arms and looked all around. "Do you see what I see?"

Two girls, identical twins, shot their arms up. "The walls?" asked one twin, Molly.

"The board?" asked the other, Holly.

"Yes and yes. The walls, the board, our classroom—everything is made of atoms and molecules. Whether you can see it or not, science is everywhere." He let out an exaggerated breath. "I just exhaled molecules that you can't see." He chortled before pointing to George. "What did you eat for breakfast?"

"Pancakes," he answered.

He moved to Olive. "And how about you?"

"Eggs, sunny side up." Snickers came from the back row.

Mr Timberlac pointed to Ivy and she stopped giggling. "What did you have?"

"A kale smoothie," she answered.

"Cooking pancakes and eggs"—he made flipping motions with his hand—"growing kale"—he crouched down, put his hands together and wiggled his way up—"they all involve chemical processes." Then he pointed to the breakdancer. "What are you doing after school?"

"Skateboarding," he answered.

Mr Timberlac pointed to a girl in the middle of class. "Shooting hoops," she said.

Then he looked right at me. "What are you doing?"

"Umm . . ." I could hear cackles from the back. "I'm still thinking about it."

He splayed his arms excitedly. "That's exactly what I'm talking about. Whether you're skateboarding, playing basketball or thinking, all sorts of physical and biological processes are occurring." Unlike any teacher I ever had, he told us he would teach the topics in no particular order. "Science is everywhere, so I am not going to categorize anything." He continued his train of questions, waving his arms and twitching his head like a music conductor.

When class was over, Olive invited me to her house to watch *Ninja Girls*.

"Let's go do something exciting instead . . ."

"What's more exciting than ninja girls kicking ass?"

"I meant let's go walk around the village or the dock."

"How's that more exciting?"

"If we're not out, how are we supposed to find out?"

"Okay, Little Miss Know-It-All, let's go!" She turned toward George. "You want to come with?"

"I've gotta get home first. My cousin just flew in today."

We convinced him to meet us at the dock later.

Olive and I wandered by the stores in the village before heading to the harbour. We slowed down as we approached Gisele's. The usual lineup curled around the corner, and we stood at the end of it. It was moving even slower than usual.

"Super exciting," said Olive in a sarcastic tone.

"Ha ha, the day's not over."

"I suppose . . . good thing I have the weekend to look forward to."

"This weekend?" I asked, hoping I'd forgotten something to look forward to.

"We have tickets for the sci-fi convention." She swung her hips and pumped her shoulders like a GIF clip.

"Who's we?"

"My parents and I . . ." Her voice trailed off. "Do you want to come? I'll see if my mom can get an extra ticket."

"No it's okay." It really wasn't my thing anyway. Plus we were in high school now. We should be doing stuff *without* parents. I mean, who needs them?

As I turned toward the water, I saw Poppy reading a book on a bench overlooking the boats. With her empty hand, she twirled her hair with a finger, kind of like Mom when she was in deep thought. Before I could even blink, Ivy and Suzy were by her side. Poppy quickly stuffed her book in her bag and pulled out her phone.

Olive waved her hand in front of my face. "So what do you think?"

"About what?"

"Joining a club outside of school, since we don't seem to agree on anything at school." She pulled out her phone. "Let's see what's out there." The second she tapped her phone, her jaw dropped. "OMG, the *Magical Creatures* TV show is filming in Steveston!" Her head scanned the boardwalk. "I wonder if we'll run into any of the stars?"

"Hey!" George hollered as he made his way toward us with another guy around our age. He had wispy curls and forest-green eyes. I recognized him but couldn't quite put a finger on it.

"You're that guy . . ." Olive didn't finish her sentence, but her rosy cheeks turned rosier.

"This is my cousin, Cole," said George. "He's staying with us for a while."

"Nice to meet you." Cole held out his fish and chips. "Want some?"

Olive convinced me to abandon the ice cream lineup, and we all made our way to a picnic bench. As soon as Cole sat down, Olive slid in beside him and rested her chin on her palm.

Just as I was going to ask Cole about moving here, George threw a fry at him. He caught it with his mouth and flung one back. After a few tosses back and forth, George launched one up high—so high that it forced Cole to leap out of his seat to catch it with his mouth. When he sat back down, "PFFFFFFFFFFFFTPPP," there was a super loud fart noise. George laughed hysterically, holding up his phone with some fart app.

"Real mature, George." Cole lobbed another fry back at him.

This time, ketchup streaked George's arm and he pretended he was shot, holding his chest and collapsing to the ground.

Everyone was watching. Everyone including Poppy.

I hoped she didn't think I was friends with these guys. *Boys can be so immature.* Even if there were a book about the science of boys, I still wouldn't understand them.

Cole had to go meet someone, but Olive, George and I stayed out until they had to go home for dinner. Before they left, Olive put her arm around me. "You were right, this was fun."

Outside the gift shop was a newsstand with a bunch of candy bars, magazines and souvenirs. I bought a chocolate bar, flipped through a teen magazine and stopped at a page with trending items: shirts with memes, wireless earphones, necklaces with a key. I wondered, *what causes something to trend?*

I felt a tap on my shoulder. "Hi."

I recognized the voice and turned around to see Poppy. The trending key necklace hung around her neck.

My jaw stiffened. "I really am sorry about . . ."

"Oh whatever." She waved it off. "How do you know Cole James?" Before I could even answer, she rambled on. "If my friends found out I was hanging out with him, they'd freak out!"

"With Cole?" I couldn't understand.

"Yeah, the guy in the stretchy cheese commercial. *Stretcheeeeesy.*" She pulled away from her mouth with her hand.

Oh that's where I'd seen him.

"He's got like thousands of followers," she said. "Anyway, I waved to him, but he didn't wave back. Ivy and Suzy told me you're a nerd. That means you're smart, right? Do you think you could help me get his attention?"

My mouth dropped open. Why would she need my help? But I also felt a twinge of joy, like I'd just eaten a piece of chocolate. "I guess I could introduce you."

"I have to make a good first impression. I *need* to stand out."

I was going to tell her that she already stood out because she was so pretty, but I decided against it—I didn't want to seem desperate for friends.

There was a long silence. "Well?" she prompted.

I thought back to the fart incident with Cole and George. "I'm writing a book about the science of boys." The words flew out of my mouth.

Poppy's eyes widened. "Really? Can I read it?"

Huh? Wait! My heart pounded. *What did I just get myself into?* I was neck deep in water. "Well . . . I'm not finished yet." *Why can't I stop talking?*

"It's okay, I could just start reading the first chapter."

My mind went blank. I filled my lungs with air and held my breath . . . but I was sinking.

Then she said, "If you help me, I can help you with whatever *that* is." She waved her hand up and down at my outfit.

My head popped out of the water. "You could?" It was just what I needed to keep myself from drowning. "Deal," I said and shook her hand.

The only problem: *I don't know anything about boys.*

ACTIVATION BARRIER

The energy required for a chemical reaction to proceed.

Dad was in the kitchen reading a science article with a glass of orange juice in hand. I cleared my throat. "Remember you said I could have a phone when I started high school?"

He started making some notes. "I never said that."

I knew he wasn't making as much money with his new job. I'd overheard him talking to Mom about it. "I'll pay for it myself," I said.

"You're too young for a cellphone."

"But you promised!"

"No I didn't."

"Then it was Mom. Either way, I really need one."

He pointed to the beige phone hanging on the wall. I pursed my lips and picked up the phone to call Mom. Straight to voicemail. "Hi, Mom, can you please remind Dad that you promised me a phone when I started high school? Anyway, I wish you were here . . ."

Dad peered up for a moment and then down again before rubbing his eyes. They looked like they were watering.

"Talk soon." I hung up the phone. "What's wrong, Dad?"

He took out a handkerchief and blew his nose. "Just allergies." Made sense. Since Mom's been gone, our place was dustier than usual. He stared back down at the article.

I pointed to a diagram of a peak. "What's that?"

He traced the peak upward. "In order for a reaction to occur, the starting materials have to have enough energy to get over this barrier. It's like the energy you need to climb a mountain."

"Speaking of barriers, high school has enough of them as is. A cellphone would really help me out."

He shook his head. "Research has shown that the overuse of technology in adolescents interferes with their cognitive development. There's a reason why the bigwigs in Silicon Valley raise their kids tech-free for as long as possible."

"But this is not Silicon Valley. It's Steveston and everyone my age has a cellphone." As soon as those words fell out of my mouth, I knew I'd lost the battle. He was never one to follow a trend or do something just because other people did it. He used to encourage me to embrace my uniqueness, and I'd believed him, but now I wasn't so sure. He also used to make me laugh, pretending the kitchen was a lab, synthesizing the most delicious meals. Now he sat with a piece of meat on his plate that was so dehydrated I couldn't even tell what it was.

I was wasting my time. I had a bigger mountain to climb. *What can I write in this so-called book of mine?*

I went to Dad's office to use his computer. Piles of folders were stacked everywhere, and papers covered the floor like tiles. I cleared his desk, opened a new document and

started typing. *"The thing about boys is that . . ."* Clicking my tongue several times, I hoped the answer would roll off, but it didn't.

I decided to do some research and typed "science of boys" in the search bar. Scrolling through the results, I found a video of a young boy performing science experiments, a book about how to raise sons and an article about how STEM is for everyone, not just boys. Nothing about how to get a boy's attention.

For some inspiration, I gazed up at an old sun-bleached poster on the wall with cartoon sketches of the world's most famous scientists: Albert Einstein writing $E = mc^2$ in a notebook, Sir Isaac Newton eating an apple, Marie Curie pouring the contents of a test tube into a flask, and a dozen more geniuses.

What did each of these scientists have in common? I peered up at the poster again to see that several of the scientists were writing notes.

They all had notebooks. Plus I'd read in a study that the mind is more engaged when words are written out physically.

I took out a pen and my favourite notebook from Dad. Each page had C Ho Co La Te written at the top with symbols of the periodic table and was covered with chocolate bar squares. *"Boys are ... "* I don't know. *"Boys act the way they do because..."*

"Ugh!" I smacked my forehead with the palm of my hand. How was I supposed to write a chapter about the

science of boys, let alone a whole book? At this rate, it was going to take me *forever*.

A good night's rest was supposed to help with problem solving, so I went to bed. But I tossed and turned all night and woke up with nothing but cold sweats. I'd gotten myself into a mess, and I needed to find a way out.

Maybe I could ask Dad for his scientific opinion. He was a scientist after all . . . and at one time he was a boy.

He lay stretched out on the couch in the living room. I was surprised to see him still in his pyjamas. "Dad, don't you have to get to work?"

"One of the perks of my new job is that it's closer to home, so I have more time." His words were upbeat but his tone fell flat. Why couldn't he just admit he missed his old job? He had no problem spending long hours there.

"So, Dad, what made you fall in love with Mom?"

His face turned pale.

"Are you okay?"

"Oh buckyballs. Just realized the time." He got up quickly and left the room.

"Told you to get ready for work," I hollered. "Who's the adult around here?"

"Breakfast is on the stove," he shouted back.

I plunked a large spoonful of oatmeal into a bowl along with a piece of chocolate. It wouldn't melt, so I pulled the chocolate back out, licked off the oatmeal and let it melt in my mouth.

It got me thinking. How does one melt the heart of another? *Heat melts things.* Maybe Poppy could blast Cole with a hair dryer . . . now I was going cuckoo.

Focus. I thought back to the scientists on the wall. What did they write in their notebooks?

Observations!

I packed up my C Ho Co La Te notebook and headed to school. I paid extra attention to the guys in class. Head-bopper guy from homeroom played drums on his knees. Another guy played video games on his phone. I watched one guy take his gum out and stick it to the bottom of his desk.

In the halls, breakdancer guy practised some sort of move. While the video gamer from class was doing something on his laptop, I slowly passed behind him and saw he was writing code or something. Another guy with slightly longer hair was brushing it back with his hand, only to mess it up again. He kept repeating this cycle over and over. Maybe his head was itchy. Hair guy stopped mid-comb when Poppy, Ivy and Suzy walked by. "What's up?" He cocked his head.

As Poppy turned in my direction, I dashed away. I still didn't have anything to give her. I hid under the stairwell, pulled out my notebook and made some notes. *"Boys are simple creatures."* I crossed out *simple* and replaced it with *complex. "Boys are complex creatures. They are difficult to understand. They like chewing gum. They like music, video games and their hair."* Arrgh! Anybody could like these things, not just boys.

Who was I kidding? I had no idea what I was doing. I imagined telling Poppy, "Sorry, I lied. I actually can't help you." I felt sick to my stomach.

CHAPTER 5

CATALYST

A substance that speeds up a reaction by lowering the activation barrier.

After school Olive came up to me with a smile as big as the sun. "Cole's in the *Magical Creatures* TV series. Can you believe it?"

"Really?" I wondered if Poppy knew. "George didn't mention anything."

"I'm just so excited they're filming here." Her smiled stretched wider. "Wanna come over? We could watch the movie again—get us ready for the TV show."

"Not today."

Her lips puckered. "What's up with you lately?"

"Nothing. I'm just trying to figure something out."

"Like what?"

"I'm trying to decode the science of . . ." I stopped mid-sentence. Olive wouldn't understand. "The science of chocolate. Why it's so addictive." I pulled out two pieces of chocolate and gave her one.

She unwrapped it and popped it in her mouth. "Fine. I know how you get when you have something on your mind."

"You're so understanding." I grinned and ate my piece.

In a last-ditch effort to come up with something to write for the science of boys, I went for a walk. Studies showed that walking stimulates the growth of new neurons, which in turn stimulate new ideas.

I found myself back at the harbour. Seagulls squawked and swooped above me. I felt like any minute I was going to get pooped on, so I walked down to Fisherman's Wharf to shield myself under the tarp awnings attached to the boats. The smell of raw seafood and boat engine exhaust filled the air. Saul the sea lion was out, making his rounds about the boats.

"Fresh salmon, fresh shrimp!" an old lady hollered. Distracted, I stepped on something gooey. I lifted my shoe to see some mustard-coloured goop. Above me, a sign read SEA URCHIN.

As I rubbed the sole of my shoes on a wooden ledge, I heard a voice.

"Gum or dog poop?" It was Cole.

"Neither, thank goodness." I showed him the bottom of my shoe. "Sea urchin."

He pretended to gag. "I'd take gum or poop over sea urchin any day."

"Are you serious? Gum is impossible to remove, and dog poop—did you know just a gram of it contains over twenty million fecal coliform bacteria?"

A peculiar smile appeared on his face, and I changed the subject. "What are you up to anyway?"

He pointed to the distance where a bunch of people scurried around a large camera and white screen.

"That's right, you're in the new *Magical Creatures* TV show. I guess that's why you're staying with George?"

"Yeah, my mom wanted me to stay with family."

"Where are you from originally?"

"We travel all over the place, but actually from here. Before we moved away, I went to daycare with George."

Wait a minute. I went to daycare with George. All of a sudden an image of a little kid hanging around a young George popped into my mind. "You didn't by chance have a shark stuffie, did you?"

His eyebrows crinkled. "How would you know that?"

"I was in that same daycare."

"You must have a really good memory." He smirked.

"What are the chances?" Wait, this was *my chance* to find out more about Cole—for Poppy. "So how long are you here for?"

"Filming is scheduled till the end of the year."

"Are you going to school or homeschooling?"

"Going to Minato High—same as you. My parents didn't want me to miss too much school 'cause I'm already behind."

"How come I haven't seen you there?"

"I'm only there when I'm not filming." Before I could ask him another question, Cole said he needed to get back on set. I waved to him and found myself an empty bench across from Shady Island.

Now that I knew a little more about Cole, I felt more confident. He was going to school with us. That could help Poppy. Or maybe not. Suddenly I felt more pressure.

I wrote in my notebook, *"The Science of Boys . . ."* and nervously tapped my finger on the page—I still had nothing.

"Emma!"

I jumped out of my seat. "You scared me, George. What are you doing here?"

"I walked here with Cole." He took a swig of his frothy drink.

"What's that?"

"Protein shake." He puffed out his chest, flexed a bicep and deepened his voice. "I'm getting huge. Want some?"

"Does it have dairy?"

"It's made with milk."

"No thanks, I don't make enough lactase." At his confused look, I explained. "It's the enzyme that helps break down lactose. The catalyst that speeds up the digestion of dairy." His face was still blank. "I'm lactose intolerant."

"Why didn't you just say so?" He took another swig. "So what's up? You looked like you were thinking really hard about something."

"It's nothing."

He snatched my notebook and stood up with his arm in the air. "What's *this*, then?"

I jumped up. "Give it back!"

He glanced at the open page. "Science of boys, eh?"

I hopped on the bench, grabbed my notebook and clutched it to my chest. "It's none of your business." As I glared at George, something dawned on me. "You're a boy . . ."

"You just noticed now?"

I wasn't getting anywhere on my own. I needed to talk to someone . . . the words tumbled out of my mouth. "I told Poppy that I could help her with Cole."

He looked intrigued. "Poppy Sinclair?"

"I'm supposed to be writing a book about the science of boys, but I have no clue what I'm doing."

He downed the rest of his shake. "I'll help you."

"How?" My hands landed on my hips.

"Cole's my cousin. I could tell you everything you need to know about him."

"Why didn't you tell me he's in the *Magical Creatures* TV show?"

"Cole's kind of private. He didn't want me to go around announcing it."

"So you know stuff about him that nobody else knows?"

"Of course. I live with the guy."

An idea started forming like a reaction product. George was exactly what I needed to help me write my book. He was the . . . "Catalyst!" I said excitedly. "You're my catalyst!"

His eyebrows scrunched.

"You could help me."

"That's what I said." A smug smile appeared on his face. I huffed. "What do you want?"

"Nothing. Friends help friends, right?" He feathered his bangs up higher than they were.

A big weight suddenly lifted off my shoulders. For the first time since I made the promise to Poppy, I didn't feel lost. I was motivated like a fish ready to swim upstream.

CHAPTER 6

THE LAW of
UNIVERSAL GRAVITATION

Every particle is attracted to every other particle in the universe.

George and I agreed to meet early the next morning at
Garry Point, a park midway between our houses. I was
extra early, so I went for a walk on the pathway above the
beach. It circled around a large open field. As I waited for
George, I watched several kites sail above me in the wind.
The breeze chilled me, and I wrapped my coat, dotted with
lambs, tightly around my body. It was soft and comforting.

I heard a rustling and turned to see George chewing on
a breakfast bar. "Do you want one?"

"I'm okay. I'd rather talk about how you're going to help
me."

"I can tell you whatever you need to know about Cole."

"Like what?"

"Like what shampoo he uses and what he eats for breakfast."

"That's all great, but the book is about the science of
boys." I moaned. Maybe this was a bad idea.

"Tell me something science-y and I'll give you some
advice, from a guy's perspective."

As I looked around, a little girl appeared with her dad and what looked like a homemade butterfly kite made of nylon. She started running and her dad chased behind her, holding up the kite before throwing it up in the air. A gust of wind caught it, and the butterfly surged upward. For several seconds it soared through the air wild and free.

Just as quickly, the wind disappeared and the kite came crashing down.

"Gravity!" I blurted. "The law of universal gravitation states that every thing in the universe is attracted to every other thing, and the force between them is proportional to their masses but inversely proportional to the square of their distance."

George narrowed his eyes. "What are you talking about?"

"What goes up must come down."

"Why didn't you just say that?" He rubbed his chin, then paused. "Get Poppy to throw something up at Cole and see if he catches it."

How was that going to work? Then I remembered Cole and George throwing french fries back and forth at each other. Maybe George was on to something.

I pulled out my C Ho Co La Te notebook and jotted down some notes. *"If you like a guy but he doesn't know you exist, you have to get his attention. If you don't want to make it too obvious, use the forces of gravity to help you."* I wrote about the universal law of gravity: *"The gravitational force between two objects is directly related to their masses and..."* No, this was too confusing. I crossed out the last part.

"The gravitational force between two masses is stronger if they're heavier. That's why everything gets pulled toward the planet's centre—Earth is massive. That's why an object that goes up gets pulled down." Don't get carried away with the science. Focus on the guy.

"The good news: You can use this to your advantage. Throw something up toward the guy of your affection, and let gravity do its job. Whatever you throw at him is bound to come down, forcing his attention."

George and I made a plan to meet near the stairwell at recess. He told me he was going to show Cole around school.

At recess I found Poppy by her locker, reading a book with a cherry-topped pie on the cover. She wore a white shirt, jean shorts and a pair of grey kicks, all so simple and yet so stylish. Before I could say anything ...

"Hey, Books, I was looking for you."

She gave me a nickname. *And she likes reading—this must be a good sign.* I was thrilled but played it cool. "Did you hear that Cole's in the *Magical Creatures* TV series?"

"Really? What? There was nothing on his social media about it." She put down her book, grabbed her phone and swiped, tapped and scrolled. "You're right, he's listed as a cast member." Then she slammed her locker shut. "You know what this means, right?"

I shrugged.

"I have to get his attention before everyone else finds out." Her voice dropped. "So, what's the plan?"

I opened my C Ho Co La Te notebook, ripped out the pages and handed her my notes. "*Ding*," I said, since I didn't have a phone.

Her nose scrunched up. Then she read the note and looked even more confused. "So, you want me to throw something at Cole? I'm not sure about this."

I remembered that Poppy was at the dock when Cole and George were launching french fries at each other. "Guys like to chuck things at each other, like fries."

She nodded very slowly, like a memory stirred in her mind. "I don't know . . ."

"At the very least he's going to have to give back whatever you throw at him." I led her to the hallway, above the stairs, where George and I had agreed to meet. George wasn't there, but Cole stood near the bottom of the stairs. "And did you hear he goes to our school?"

Poppy's eyes nearly popped out of their sockets when she saw Cole. Circling him were several girls, giggling and playing with their hair. Word was already out that he was in the TV series. Two more girls approached him, and Poppy's lips tightened. "Okay I'll do it. But how do I get to him with all those other girls?"

Where the heck was George? I could hear my heart thumping and had to do something. I went down the stairs, manoeuvred around the crowd and grasped Cole by the arm. "Can you come with me?"

He let out a huff. "Thanks, Emma. I was feeling claustrophobic."

"Where's George?"

"I don't know."

"I thought George was supposed to show you around . . ." Before I could finish my sentence, more people began to approach him. I pointed toward the stairwell, and Cole followed me.

As we climbed the stairs, I gave Poppy a discreet thumbs up, signalling her. At first she hesitated . . . but then she must have seen the swarm of girls encroaching. She pulled off her shoe and flung it in the air.

The shoe went up . . . and then came down. I quickly moved out of the way.

"Ouch!" Cole yelped and I turned away. What if he was hurt? She's going to be embarrassed . . . furious . . . at me.

With jaw clenched, I slowly rotated my head toward Cole. He didn't seem upset. He picked up the shoe, looking around. "Whose is this?"

"It's mine," a girl wearing a flower headband hollered.

Another girl, in a plaid skirt, shoved her out of the way. "No it's mine."

Even head-bopper guy claimed the shoe was his.

Poppy cleared her throat. "Actually it belongs to me." She raised her foot with the other shoe as everyone looked up at her.

Cole finished climbing the stairwell and passed the shoe to Poppy. She gazed at him like he was the only star in the sky.

I looked at Cole's facial expression. Did he look happy? Did he feel anything for Poppy? I couldn't tell. The next thing I knew, a stream of girls went up the stairs and barraged him.

Poppy ran down to me. "Eek, that really worked! I was like a modern-day Cinderella. Did you see everyone looking at us?" She pulled out her phone. "I should have got you to take a pic of us." She held the shoe to her face and took a selfie. "Prince Charming strikes," she said as she tapped her phone.

She kicked off her other shoe and handed me the pair. "Here, Books, put these on. The first rule to dressing chic: Don't wear anything with holes in it, except ripped jeans, knitted sweaters and sandals." She pulled out a pair of flip-flops and slid them on.

I took off my sneakers and put on Poppy's kicks. They fit perfectly. In that moment my cloud of gloom parted, and I swirled around like a kite flying on the windiest of days.

Then I heard chuckles and opened my eyes. Ivy was pointing to a little lamb on my coat, pretending to hold in her laugh. "Did you get this from a baby store?" Suzy joined in and Poppy turned the other way.

Just like that, my kite came crashing down.

DUAL NATURE OF LIGHT

Light behaves like a wave and a particle.

Later that day I found George in the hallway. "Where were you? You almost sabotaged our plan." I would have been more annoyed except for the fact that his advice actually worked. "Luckily, I managed to get Cole near Poppy."

"You did?" He raised an eyebrow. "How'd it go?"

"It worked, no thanks to you."

"Oh it did. I mean, yeah, obviously." His mouth twitched. George didn't seem as excited as I was, but I guess he was only doing me a favour.

The bell rang, and we walked to English class together. I knew from my timetable that we had Godzilla as our teacher, and I warned George. "I had her for homeroom and she's really strict." George already knew her nickname and told me he'd heard rumours about her.

The desks in our classroom were organized in groups of four. George went to sit with coding guy and gum guy. I headed toward an empty seat near the window and stared out at the leaves' bright autumn colours.

Breakdancer guy and hair guy seemed to have hit it off. They quickly turned their heads when Poppy, Ivy and Suzy pranced in. Breakdancer guy cocked his head, and hair guy flicked his hair, messing it up and combing it out again.

Ivy turned to me and muttered, "Bah, bah," like a lamb. Suzy copied her.

I sat dead still until Olive came in and glared at them. "What are you laughing at?"

"Here's mama sheep protecting her little baby," Ivy along with Suzy mocked. I glanced over at Poppy, who peered down without a word. I couldn't understand. I thought Poppy and I were becoming friends.

Olive clanked my wrist with hers. "Cole goes to our school! Everyone's talking about it."

I acted surprised.

"There's a cast autograph signing to promote the TV show! We've gotta go!"

"Sure," I said.

"You don't sound excited . . . it's going to be unbelievable. All the main characters are going to be there including Wentworth the Wizard and Empress Octavia."

"And Cole!" Molly and Holly said simultaneously as they slid into the seats across from us.

"Can you believe we're going to school with a celebrity?" said Molly.

"He's so cute," said Holly.

Just then, Cole came in and gasps swept the air. He sat down across from George.

Olive gazed over at them. "I can't believe George didn't tell us anything about him."

"Cole seems like a pretty private person," I said.

"I wonder what else George is hiding. He seems kind of secretive lately."

"Errr . . . I don't think so at all. George reads like an open book."

Godzilla lumbered in, and the noise dropped the way it does moments before the start of a surprise party. Her hair was combed back in the usual bun without a single hair out of place. She stood in front of the class with her neck extended and glasses tipped down. Without introducing herself, she got straight to the point. "As the media has a significant influence on our society and our thinking, I want you to find an example of misrepresentation in the media and present the truth to the rest of us."

"Can we work in partners?" Molly and Holly asked in unison.

"You may work with a partner or in small groups."

The twins smiled at each other. Poppy seemed to have formed a group with Ivy and Suzy, who sat across from her. Ivy wore a pretentious smile. Olive turned to me, pointing at herself then to me, and I gave her a thumbs up.

Godzilla scattered a stack of magazines and newspapers around the classroom and gave us some time to work on the project. Olive flipped through an issue of *Steveston Scoop* before stopping at a page. "It says here there's going to be some sort of contest for local fans at the *Magical Creatures'* signing. Eek, I wonder what it could be?"

Godzilla stumped toward us. "Less gossip, more work."

Olive skimmed through the pages of a fashion magazine, turning each page faster and faster before moaning. "There isn't a single girl in here who's bigger than a size two."

I came across an article titled "It's Not the Size You're In, It's the Confidence Within" and handed it to her. "You need to be reading more articles like this."

But as I flipped through another teen magazine, I couldn't help noticing that she was right. We were bombarded with images of girls who were not only thin, they were also beautiful with perfect hair and perfect skin. *How is any normal person able to compete with that?* I thought about it. "Maybe we could talk about the misrepresentation of girls in the media?"

"What do you mean?"

"Look at these girls! They're all gorgeous. It's not real life."

"You're so right. Come to think of it, the four girls who play the main characters in *Ninja Girls* are all models in real life."

"That's what I mean! They don't cast ordinary girls."

I heard giggling . . . it came from the corner where Poppy, Ivy and Suzy sat, their heads huddled together.

"I wonder what they're talking about?" I said.

"Why do you care?"

"Look at them. They're always so . . ." I couldn't think of the right word to describe them . . . except . . . "sparkly."

"Like this?" Olive wiggled her index finger with a fake diamond ring.

"Cubic zirconia?"

She looked defensive. "What's wrong with cubic zirconia?"

"Nothing, I guess."

"Well you know how I feel?" Olive said. "When you hang out with good-looking people, you look less attractive."

"Huh?"

"You *sparkle* more if you hang out with people who are less sparkly, not more."

Godzilla walked by us clicking her tongue.

I pulled out my C Ho Co La Te notebook and pretended to make notes. I ended up drawing a diamond. With my pencil I made streaks over and over it. *What makes someone sparkle?*

The pinky side of my hand got marked up by the pencil streaks. *Ugh.* I rubbed my hand on a blank part of the paper. Then I paused. I studied the carbon stain on my hand and then the picture of the diamond.

Pencil lead is made of carbon . . .

So are diamonds.

If something as dull as pencil lead is made of the same thing as diamonds . . .

I still have hope.

After class I said hi to Poppy on her way out. She turned away like she hadn't heard me and said something to Ivy and Suzy. But later in the hallway she pulled me aside. "Books, I waved to Cole, even raised my foot to remind him of the shoe he returned to me, but no response."

I remembered something. "There's a signing to promote the *Magical Creatures* TV show. Cole will be there."

She looked right at me. "I guess we're going then."

I was so excited we were finally getting somewhere. But as soon as Ivy and Suzy walked toward us, she gave me the cold shoulder again. Her attitude changed like the colours of the autumn leaves.

In science, Mr Timberlac sprinted in. "Like the speed of light," he huffed and flickered the lights on and off. He had on a split suit. One half was patterned with waves and the other half had tiny polka dots. He wrote "Wave-particle duality" on the board. "Light is unique. It behaves as both a wave," he said while doing some kind of wave motion with his arm, "and a particle." He dotted the air with his fingers.

My eyes met Poppy's, so I gave her a small wave. She waved back but instantly turned away when Ivy said something to her.

I stared down at my notes. *"The dual nature of light . . ."* I crossed out *light* and replaced it with *Poppy.*

CHAPTER 8

KINETIC MOLECULAR THEORY

Everything is made up of molecules that are constantly moving.

The next day I waited for George at his locker. He finally came, wearing a broad-shouldered suit jacket. "Hey, how do I look in this?"

"I'm not sure what you want me to say."

"Suits are supposed to make your shoulders and chest look bigger."

"I have more important things to talk to you about. What do I tell Poppy . . ."

Before I could finish, gum guy and coding guy interrupted us and we walked to science together. Molly and Holly were already there, and Poppy sauntered in with Ivy and Suzy. Poking out of Poppy's bag was a book with a fish on the cover. Breakdancer guy and hair guy came in pretty much at the same time and sat beside them. The five of them took over the back row.

Right as the bell rang, Olive came in and sat next to me and George. "Geek squad together again," Ivy jeered, and giggles followed. Olive turned around, presumably to give her a dirty look. George didn't say a word. He actually looked a bit nervous. Then Cole strolled in and the murmurs began. Our eyes met and he gave me a little head nod.

"Cole, come sit with us," said Molly and Holly, who sat in the middle of class.

"I don't like to be crowded," he said and took a seat in the front row.

A glass of ice water and a mug of something steaming sat at the front of class. Mr Timberlac's arms flailed as his head bobbled. "All molecules move. Depending on if the molecules are in a solid," he fished out an ice cube, "liquid," he dipped his finger in the water, "or gas," he blew the steam

coming out of the mug, "molecules behave differently." He held up an image of the three main states of matter: solid, liquid and gas. Then he told the first two rows to stand up. "You're the solid molecules. Get closer together." Right away the girls in the front flocked toward Cole. I could hear the "no fair" sighs from the middle and back of the room. Mr Timberlac pointed to the middle two rows. "You're the liquid molecules. Please take one step apart from each other." Then he pointed to the last two rows, which we were in. "The molecules in the gas state are even farther apart. Please take two steps back."

Poppy kept an eye on Cole. Hair guy and breakdancing guy had their eyes on Poppy. George kept looking back and forth between Cole and Poppy. I was glad to see he was taking his role as catalyst seriously.

Mr Timberlac explained that molecules in the solid state have the least amount of energy while molecules in the gas state have the greatest amount of energy. He asked the students in the solid group to stay where they were with little motion, which made the girls surrounding Cole grin. He told the students in the liquid group to move around a little more. Then he told us, the gas group, to "Jiggle and wiggle everywhere."

I was embarrassed to jiggle and wiggle. I stretched out my arms and pretended to yawn. Everyone else danced up a storm, well, except George; he looked a little lost, especially because he was next to Poppy, who moved so effortlessly.

As we danced, Poppy pulled me to the corner. "Should I go up to Cole?"

I shuffled toward George and whispered, "Should Poppy dance near Cole?"

"No," he said abruptly.

My eyebrows raised.

"Look, if Poppy wants Cole to get moving, tell her to stay away from him."

"What? You make no sense."

"Molecules move faster when they're farther apart." He pointed to the image of the gas state.

He's right.

"Look, he doesn't like crowds, so you could see how girls who are too forward could be a turnoff."

Cole had said "I don't like to be crowded" when Molly and Holly asked him to sit with them in the middle of class. I guessed George knew what he was talking about.

I scooched back to Poppy. "You better wait. I'll get you the next chapter."

Poppy's attention shifted toward Ivy and Suzy, who were busy chatting. Then she dropped her voice. "Books, where's a quiet place we could meet?"

I knew the perfect place and told her about Maritime Anytime. I'd never seen anyone from school there.

Maritime Anytime was a local bookstore on a small side street in Steveston village. I pushed the ship's steering wheel on the door to open it. Immediately the smell of coffee, wood and old books came pouring out.

I knew Poppy would love it here as much as I did. The twelve-foot high walls were covered from floor to ceiling with books, the centre shelves were arranged like a labyrinth and the café was nestled snugly in the back with vintage maps, anchors and model ships.

I pulled out my C Ho Co La Te notebook and summarized the kinetic molecular theory. *"Molecules are in constant motion. They behave differently depending on whether they are in a solid, liquid or gas state."* I stretched my neck. *"Advice two: If a guy takes his time, but you want him to move quicker, stay far away from him. Like molecules in the gas phase, boys move faster when you give them space."*

The door clanged and Poppy walked in. "Wow, this place is amazing!" She looked around like she was in an art gallery. "I could spend my life here, surrounded by all these books." She zipped toward a shelf with a sign that read NEW RELEASES. After flipping through several books, she came back with one that had a kid carrying a notebook on the cover.

I propped up my glasses. "Have you always liked reading?"

"Yeah. Ever since my dad brought me back my first book after a business trip. Now he brings me a new book every time he goes away. He has a knack for finding my favourites." Then she looked at me. "He's actually a nerd like you." The way she said *nerd* made it sound like it was a compliment.

"My dad's a nerd too," I said.

"What does he do?"

"He's a chemist. He used to read science textbooks to me as bedtime stories." This made Poppy smile. I liked it better when it was just the two of us.

"So what's the next step?" she asked.

I ripped out my notes and passed them to her. *"Ding!"*

Her nose scrunched. "Why do you do that?"

"I don't have a phone."

"Well don't do it. It's weird." She was quiet as she read for a few moments. "So . . . I don't do anything?" She tapped her dimples. "I don't know about this. It's not like me to just stand around and do nothing."

Then I remembered something. "You said you wanted to stand out! He's always surrounded. What better way to stand out than to be outside the crowd?"

"You've got a point, Books." She agreed to give it a shot.

George better know what he's doing.

DIFFUSION

Diffusion is the movement of molecules from an area of high concentration to an area of low concentration.

The *Magical Creatures'* signing took place in front of Britannia Shipyards, an old wooden structure above a marsh. By the time I got there, huge crowds were aggregating like magnetic particles. People dressed as trolls, goblins and fairies traversed the platform surrounding the building.

As soon as Olive and I got in the autograph line, several others jumped in immediately behind us. We waved to Molly and Holly, who joined the line in pixie costumes. Coding guy was also there, dressed as Wentworth the Wizard, with another guy in a troll costume.

Olive, dressed as Empress Octavia in a black body suit, posed with one leg bent in front of the other, arms stretched out to the sides.

"What are you doing?"

"Yoga. I'm strengthening my core." Her cape made of a scarf slipped off onto her arms as she rotated her torso. "The Steveston ninja club is having an open house tomorrow. Let's go check it out!"

"Ninja club?" It didn't sound as exciting as she made it seem.

"You know the girl who plays Empress Octavia? Before she scored her role, she was taking ninja classes at the same time as acting lessons."

"I'm not sure . . ."

"Just come to the open house."

I glanced at my watch as I was meeting Poppy soon. "Sure, okay." Maybe Olive would want to come with me? "What do you think of Poppy Sinclair?"

"I don't really know her." She tilted her upper body down like a hand on a clock.

"I was just about to . . ." I began to say.

"She's already hanging out with Ivy and Suzy, so clearly we have nothing in common."

"She's nothing like Ivy and Suzy."

"How would you know?"

"Just a feeling." My mind drifted. "Doesn't something about her remind you of my mom?"

"Oh this is about your mom?" She flicked back up. "Why don't you just ask her?"

"Ask her what?"

"If she's coming home?"

"Of course she is." My words boomed unexpectedly. "Why do you assume she's not?" I could still hear the last thing Mom said to me before she left: "See you soon, Emma."

A hint of pity appeared on Olive's face, and my fists tightened till my knuckles were white.

Olive crouched down to another position, palms together, eyes closed. I decided it wasn't a good idea to bring her with me. Poppy might think she's weird. She might think I'm weird too if she knew we were best friends. Plus Olive made it clear she had no interest in Poppy.

The line was moving at a turtle's pace. I could go meet Poppy and then get back in line with Olive. "I'm going to get a drink," I said.

"I'll come with."

"The line's getting really long. You better hold our spot." I dashed off.

When I got to our meeting spot in front of Murakami House, I was a minute late and Poppy wasn't there. My heart sped up by the second. *I hope I didn't miss her already.*

Several minutes later I spotted Poppy in the crowd, wearing a jean jacket. I looked down at my lamb-y coat, the same one Ivy and Suzy had made fun of. Even though it was chilly, I took it off and wrapped it around my waist.

Poppy snapped photos like a photographer, pausing to tinker with her phone every few seconds. When she saw me, she waved and gestured toward the crowd. "Have you seen Cole?"

"Not yet." As we walked around, Poppy either focused on her phone or scanned the crowd. "So what sort of things do you like doing?" I asked.

"I post my favourite outfits on Instagram, but I'm not getting as many likes or followers as I want. So I started taking pics of events too, like this one." She snapped a few more photos.

"I noticed you like books. What are you reading now?" I asked.

Her head stopped turning. "I started . . ." *Ding*. Her phone interrupted and she tapped her screen. "Shoot, there's a pop-up shop happening right now. It's so hard to be in two places at once."

I know what you mean.

"I used to read more. But now I'm so busy. Social media is like a vacuum, it sucks away all your time." Her eyes darted back to her phone.

"I was thinking of joining Facebook . . . "

"Oh, Books, Facebook's ancient." She flicked on her phone and showed me a bunch of apps she uses: one with a camera, one with a music note, another with a phantom and a few others with letters or abbreviations as logos. Half of them I didn't even recognize.

"I was going to open an Instagram account but I don't have a phone, so it's kind of pointless. I wouldn't be able to take photos or post . . ." I could tell she wasn't really listening to me.

Poppy motioned with her arm. "Let's go line up!"

I didn't want to risk Olive seeing me with Poppy. "Remember what I said about standing out from the crowd?" I directed my arm to an open space in the distance. "Why don't we go stand over there?"

Her attention went back and forth between her phone and the masses of people. Her jaw dropped suddenly. "There's Cole! I'm gonna go say hi." Within seconds she disappeared into the throng.

I dashed back to the lineup, which hadn't moved much, but everyone seemed thrilled about something. When Olive saw me, she jumped up. "They announced the contest! The winner gets to meet the TV cast of *Magical Creatures!*" She grabbed her cheeks. "I have to win. I'll die if I don't."

"Aren't you being a little dramatic?"

She gave me an imploring smile.

"Let me guess—you want me to enter so that your chances are higher?"

Olive hugged me before doing her happy dance. "The contest is only for diehard local fans at this event, so the odds are good. Fairies with ballots are supposed to be flying around . . . there!" She pointed.

One came down the line with shimmering wings and a box that read ENTER TO WIN.

When the fairy came to us, Olive immediately filled out a ballot and asked for another one.

"One per person," said the fairy through glittering lipstick.

"It's for my friend." Olive elbowed me.

The fairy handed me a ballot and I filled it out.

"Where's our drinks, Emma?"

Shoot, I forgot. "Be right back." On the way to the juice truck, Molly and Holly waved to me . . . in goblin costumes. "Weren't you dressed as pixies earlier?" I asked.

"We changed," said Molly and Holly at the same time.

"We wanted to enter the contest again," said Molly.

"The fairies are being strict about the one per person policy," said Holly.

Just as I approached the juice truck, another goblin hobbled right by me, blood smeared across his face. I knew it was fake. *It's just red paint.* But my head was like a helium balloon floating away. Taking a few deep breaths, I walked away from the crowd, toward the water.

I was still faint and pulled out an article from my bag. "Diffusion occurs in liquids and gases," I read. It listed everyday examples such as food dye spreading in water, perfume dispersing its smell and hot water darkening from tea leaves.

My head started to feel normal again, and I walked to the mobile drink cart on the path along the water. I got two orange sodas, one for me and one for Olive. Sipping on mine, I stared out. The sunset was unusually bright, so much so that it pleaded for attention. The breeze off the water was cool, so I pulled the lamb-y coat off my waist and put it back on.

All of a sudden I heard my name. I jumped up and spilled some soda on my coat. As I wiped it, Cole walked toward me.

"Bird poop?" he asked.

"No, orange soda." I let the tissue paper absorb the stain. "Don't tell me you prefer bird poop over orange soda."

"Well it wouldn't stain." He tilted his head. "And you'd have good luck."

"I don't believe in superstitions. I need scientific evidence."

He grinned.

"So how does it feel to be part of the biggest series ever filmed here?" I asked.

"It's a small part."

"Yeah, but in a huge production. What are you doing here anyway? Shouldn't you be with your fan club?"

"I don't want it to go to my head. It's not me they really like. It's the idea of me." His gaze shifted.

He was different from what I'd thought—not that I thought a ton about him or anything.

From the corner of my eye, I saw Poppy walking toward us. Her eyes widened as she twirled her hair.

I took a step back. "Cole, you know Poppy, right?"

"The girl with the shoe." He raised his chin and smiled. "How's it going?"

Poppy squeezed my arm and I could feel her excitement.

Before we could talk about anything else, a bunch of girls swarmed Cole and pushed us out of the way. "Could we get a photo?" a girl with blue hair shouted.

"Did you see that?" Poppy asked. "Cole smiled at me!" Then she stretched out her arm and took a selfie with Cole in the background. "How did you get him to come here?"

I didn't. "Um . . . did you enter the contest?" I asked.

"What contest?"

"To win a meet and greet with the cast of *Magical Creatures*," said a familiar voice.

I looked around to see a unicorn with four legs. Molly . . . or Holly was nestled at the front of a two-person costume.

"What? How?" Poppy pulled out her phone again.

I pointed to a fairy holding a box and a sign, and Poppy sprinted toward her. I followed. She looked at me after filling out a ballot. "What are you waiting for?"

"I already filled one out."

She pulled me aside and whispered, "Fill out another one, for me."

The fairy squinted at me. "Only one entry per person." Her face was painted so heavily with sparkles, I couldn't tell if she was the same fairy from earlier.

I met Poppy's gaze and without making eye contact with the fairy, I said, "First one for me."

She slowly handed me a form, and I quickly filled it out.

"Thanks, Books. If you win, I'll owe you big." Before I could even let out a sigh, she asked again. "So *how* did you get Cole to come over here?"

Poppy waited for an answer, and I said the first thought that seeped into my mind: "Diffusion."

"Huh?"

"Things tend to move from an area of high concentration to an area of low concentration."

Poppy's nose crinkled.

"Remember, Cole doesn't like crowds. It was only a matter of time before he took a break and escaped the masses."

"You were right." She took off her jean jacket and handed

it to me. "Your second fashion tip: don't wear clothes with stains on them, unless they're tie-dyed." I put on her jacket and shoved my lamb-y coat into my bag. Instantly I felt more stylish.

But she kept digging for info. "How do you know Cole so well anyway?"

I didn't really know him. Why did she think that? But when her eyes focused on mine, it didn't matter—she was actually paying attention to me. "Cole and I go *way* back."

Her head inched toward me. "Really?"

"We went to daycare together." She didn't need to know that I only recently figured this out.

"Shut up! Why didn't you say anything before?" Her palm was on my arm. "You must *really* know him then?"

"Yeah." I was so caught up in the moment, I couldn't stop. "He also worked with my mom. She's a makeup artist . . . for TV and film." Anything was possible. *She is a makeup artist.*

"That's so cool!" The joy in her voice triggered something inside of me. Then she said, "Let's hang out this weekend," and my dark cloud turned to cloud nine.

NUCLEAR CHAIN REACTION

A process in which the neutrons released from one reaction trigger subsequent reactions.

It was the weekend, and I woke up dreaming about hot-cakes. Fluffy Japanese pancakes, to be specific. I could almost feel them dissolving in my mouth like cotton candy. Dad used to make them every weekend with his chemistry-inspired kitchenware.

He would melt butter in a beaker on the stove, whip egg whites until they formed high peaks, then measure dairy-free milk in his Erlenmeyer flask (we're both lactose intolerant) and vanilla extract in his graduated cylinder. He'd twirl in his lab coat apron, looking through his goggles as he stirred like a wizard making a potion. He was so determined to keep up our weekly tradition that one time when we had a blackout, he retrieved his homemade Bunsen burner attached to a propane torch and continued making the hotcakes like it was no big deal.

Pancakes and a meetup with Poppy—a perfect way to start off the weekend. I went to the kitchen where Dad was reading a science journal with a reaction scheme on the cover. Hoping to inspire him, I searched the cupboards for his chemistry kitchenware.

Aha! Found them. I pulled out the large plastic container that housed the glassware and handed it to Dad. "I thought you could make us your famous hotcakes for breakfast."

"I already ate." He pointed to the stove. "There's some porridge left for you."

"I could help you make them . . ."

"Maybe another time. The porridge is probably still warm if you eat it now."

There was no point in arguing, so I scooped some into a bowl, along with a handful of chocolate chips from Dad's stash, watching them melt before taking a big spoonful.

"What are you reading?" A clump of chocolate-doused oatmeal clung to the roof of my mouth.

"Just a little history about the nuclear chain reaction, how one process leads to another."

"Kind of like a domino effect?" I asked.

"Right—when one event sets off a chain of similar events." I saw a familiar twinkle in his eyes. "When I was young, I was shy and never did anything outside my comfort zone. But one day I decided to take a chance. I demonstrated a science experiment for a talent show. One thing led to the next, and I made it all the way to the regionals, then the nationals. A prominent science professor saw me and asked me if I wanted to do a summer internship in his lab, so I did. Years later I ended up doing my PhD in his lab."

There was a pause. "It was during that time I met Mom. We fell in love, got engaged and moved in together. Every night we'd have tea and biscuits together, talking about our days. Mom always left the chocolate covered ones for me." He grinned. "I got my first real job, quickly moved up the ranks and became head director." The glimmer in his eyes faded.

"I get it. You miss your old job."

"That's not it. The hours were long, and I was barely home." He turned away, but I could tell his eyes welled up.

"Then why are you sad?"

He wiped his eyes. "My allergies are acting up again."

"Really? This very moment?"

He inhaled deeply. "Really. I enjoy what I'm doing now. I get to use my hands-on skills, I can be creative in problem solving, I get to collaborate on projects with other people, and I don't have to go to meeting after meeting talking about other meetings."

He was convincing, but I could sense he wasn't telling me the whole truth. I decided to test my theory. I went to the cupboard, took out a box of allergy medication and handed it to him. "Here, take one."

Dad shrank back and shook his head. "I'm okay."

"Research shows that antihistamines work."

He refused. "Research has also shown that they lose their effectiveness if overused."

I knew it. He needed more time to get over his job. I put away the allergy medicine and grabbed some more chocolate chips, eating a few and giving the rest to Dad. "Good news. I made a new friend at school. She's helping me with some things, and I'm helping her with other things."

Dad smiled. "That's nice."

"We're meeting at Gisele's." I placed a chocolate chip on my fingertip. "Can you believe they *still* don't have dairy-free chocolate?"

"It is hard to believe," Dad said as he walked to the sink to rinse his eyes.

I looked at the time. "Are you going to be okay?"

"I'm fine." He waved his hand behind him.

I slipped on Poppy's jean jacket and went to meet her.

As soon as I opened the door, the smell of freshly made waffle cones flooded the air. Poppy stood by the jukebox, which played an old nineties song. She fiddled with her scarf patterned with Eiffel Towers as she scrolled through the playlist.

In the corner sat a girl wearing a black shirt, her back facing me. It took me less than a picosecond to realize it was Olive. *Oh no*, I never got back in line with her at the signing.

She turned around and threw her empty cup into the bin, remnants of ice cream above her lips.

"Hey," I said.

"Where did you go yesterday?" Olive asked.

"I saw a goblin with fake blood." I pointed to her lips.

She wiped her mouth and gave me an understanding look. "You didn't feel good and went home?"

My throat strained, so I nodded and raised my arm with the DNA bracelet. She clanked it with hers.

"At least you entered the contest." She grinned. "Thanks for doing that for me."

I swatted the air like it was no big deal.

"Well let's go."

"Go where?"

She jumped into a fighting stance. "Remember the open house? Ninja club?"

Poppy approached, and for some reason I felt uneasy. "You know each other, right?"

Poppy gave Olive a smile, then went back to puttering on her phone while walking toward the gelato display.

"What are you doing with her?" Olive whispered.

"Helping her with something."

She raised an eyebrow. "With what?"

"With . . . something science related."

"So she's using you?"

"Well not exactly. Remember what I said about how important it is to dress for success. I thought maybe she could help . . ."

"So you're using her?"

"Why are you giving me such a hard time?"

"There's something about her that rubs me the wrong way." Olive's expression suddenly fell and I turned to see Ivy and Suzy.

"What are you doing here, Olive oil?" scoffed Ivy.

"Yeah, Olive oil," Suzy repeated.

"I'm not listening to the two of you. Come on, Emma. Let's go." Her bracelet jingled.

"Wait!" Poppy came back with a cone in one hand and her phone in the other. "Books, stay."

My eyes flickered back and forth between Olive and Poppy before landing back on Olive. "Um . . . I think I might stay."

"You sure?" Her eyebrows bunched together. "Suit yourself." She left but did a double take at the door before stepping outside.

Ivy and Suzy sent Poppy a puzzled look.

"Did you know that Books here's mom is a makeup artist for the movies?"

"How have I never heard this?" Ivy asked.

"Yeah, why haven't we heard this?" Suzy placed a hand on her hip.

Suddenly the room heated up and I blurted out, "She loves her job. She gets to play around with makeup all day and even gets a bunch of free samples."

Poppy inspected my face with curiosity. I'm pretty sure she was searching for any traces of makeup. "Do you get free samples?"

"Of course!" I said like it was obvious.

"What brands?" Poppy asked.

My brain spun like a centrifuge as I scanned the room for ideas. The gelato display caught my eye: chocolate, moose tracks, peaches and cream. "Momo Kesho," I uttered. "*Momo* means peach in Japanese and *kesho* is makeup."

Poppy pulled out her phone. "Momo what?" She pressed a button and the screen lit up. "I've never heard of it. How do you spell it?"

My lips trembled. "Umm . . . it's made in Japan . . . it's not very common."

To my relief, Poppy put her phone away. "Do you think I could get some free samples?"

"Me too?" asked Ivy, who I noticed for the first time wore a thick layer of foundation.

"Me three?" asked Suzy, shooting me a smile for a change.

"I don't see why not." Although I knew of many reasons why not.

"When can we get them?" Ivy asked.

"Umm . . . my mom's away right now. I'll ask her when she gets back."

"Is she on a film shoot?" Poppy asked.

I nodded.

"Cool!" said Suzy

"Where?" asked Ivy.

I scanned the display case again. Pistachio, salted caramel, french vanilla . . . "France," I said. "Paris, actually." I couldn't help it. Each lie led to the next.

ELECTROMAGNETIC SPECTRUM

A representation of the range of energies that exist.

Olive was surprisingly early to science class. She clanked her bracelet with mine and asked, "What was up the other day? Are you *friends* with Ivy and Suzy now? Never mind, obviously not. How could you be, with people who make fun of you?" She handed me a pamphlet with a ninja on it. "You've gotta join!"

Even though I wasn't as eager, I took the pamphlet.

"The workouts are gonna get us into tip-top shape." She made quick jerking movements with her arms. "Plus you'll learn all these cool moves, the kind you see in action movies."

"I don't know if it's really my thing."

She clasped her hands together. "Come to one practice. If you don't like it, I'll understand. But if you do . . ." Her eyes beamed. "Maybe one day we'll be stunt doubles."

"You know that I want to be a scientist."

"You could be a scientist who does stunts on the side. How cool would that be?"

"Okay, fine. When's practice?"

She squealed and hugged my arm. "Five pm today. Wear something comfortable. We're gonna have such a blast!"

Mr Timberlac ambled into class with symphony music blaring from an old-school stereo. All of a sudden he emitted a high-pitched tone, like he was singing opera. "ROY—G—BIV—red, orange, yellow, green, blue—" a pause, "in-di-go and vi-o-let, the colours we see—ROY—G—BIV—." He ended off on a high extended note, and eyes around me widened in amazement.

A large image of the electromagnetic spectrum spanned across the front board. "Our world consists of many types of radiation." He pointed to a narrow region labelled ROYGBIV. "Thanks to visible light, we see things. All other electromagnetic rays are invisible."

Mr Timberlac turned on his stereo, tuned it to a radio station and tapped his ear. "Radio frequency cannot be seen, yet we hear the music." He turned it off then pulled out a bag of microwave popcorn. "When we pop this, we don't see the energy going into the kernels. Yet we end up with this." He opened the bag and scooped out a handful of fluffy popcorn before pointing outside the window. "Same with ultraviolet light. We don't see that it can damage our skin."

He divided us into groups and gave each group a tablet. Hair guy, coding guy and Olive were assigned gamma rays, head-bopper and breakdancer were X-rays, and Cole, Molly and Holly were named the UV rays. The twins glowed.

I was put in the visible spectrum group with Poppy and George. He kept staring at her like he wanted to say something, and it made me nervous. But then his face flushed, and he was surprisingly quiet. Maybe he'd eaten a protein bar that'd gone bad.

While we made notes about our spectral range, Poppy leaned in toward me. "I've stayed away from Cole like you told me, but nothing's happened since the signing." She sighed. "It's hard to sit around and do nothing when everyone else is getting to know him."

I elbowed George, and he typed something on the tablet. A bunch of images with vibrant-coloured dresses lit up on the screen, and he passed it to Poppy. As she scrolled through them, he whispered to me, "Tell her to be patient. He'll come around."

"You're not helping," I said in an equally low voice.

He tilted his head toward the screen. "Tell her to wear one of those dresses. Cole likes bright colours."

"So make herself seen?"

George gave me a thumbs up and glanced over at Poppy. I pulled out my C Ho Co La Te notebook. *"It's true that guys like their space, but it's important to make sure he sees you from time to time. Advice three: make sure to stay in his visible spectrum."*

I ripped the page out and gave it to Poppy. She peered up from the screen to read it, but she didn't seem dazzled. "I really don't know why I can't just go up to Cole."

"Just think how much fun you'll have picking out the perfect outfit. You could wear it for the media presentations."

Her face lit up. "Come shopping with me after school."

Then I lit up.

Unfortunately, Ivy and Suzy came too. We went to Gisele's first. As we stood in line, Poppy swiped through her phone. "*Magical Creatures* TV already has a huge following! They haven't even aired yet." Ivy and Suzy wrapped around her to see the screen.

Once we got to the counter, Poppy ordered mint chocolate chip in a waffle cone, and Suzy ordered a scoop of bubble gum also in a cone.

"Are you five, Suze?" Ivy mocked before ordering espresso flavour in a cup. A stiff smile surfaced on Suzy's face.

As usual, the chocolate gelato stared me in the eyes. The last thing I wanted was to have to rush to the toilet, so I opted for the peach sorbet.

We sat at a booth and Ivy immediately complained. "The baby is driving me crazy. She keeps me up at night. My spare room's being invaded by toys, and I never get a say anymore—I'm like invisible." She stuck her tongue out.

"Have you talked to your mom about this?" The words just came out of my mouth.

"She said *I* have to deal with it 'cause I'm older." She shot me a glower as if I were the baby.

"At least your parents leave you alone," said Suzy. "My parents are always on my case, especially about my grades."

"If you ever need any help . . ." I said.

Ivy slid her head between us. "We'll keep that in mind."

"Ugh!" Poppy looked up from her phone. "Just missed a sample sale." Then she thumbed through her phone. "Perfect! Indigo Tree in Steveston is having a sale. Let's go."

Three elegantly dressed mannequins stood in the window display, designer clothes hung from the upper walls, and handbags dangled from the tree in the centre of the store.

Suzy pulled out a dress and handed it to Poppy. "This would look great on you."

Immediately, Ivy shoved another dress between them. "This one's much better." Poppy took both.

An iridescent dress caught my eye. Something about the colour drew me in, a mélange of purple, blue and pink, one colour standing out more depending on which angle it was viewed from. Poppy must have seen me staring at it. "Books, try it on. It'll look great on you!" I took it and went into a fitting room.

The next thing I knew, Poppy threw in a bunch of other things for me to try on. A patterned romper, ripped jeans, a fitted top and a black track suit. I swirled on my tippy-toes and even made some fashion runway expressions in the mirror . . . except I looked weird, and stopped.

Next I tried on the black track suit and jumped into a stance. *Oh no . . . Olive's class.* I quickly changed and looked at the time. It was already halfway done. I just need- ed to get there to show my face. But I had to leave now.

Poppy came out of a fitting room and asked me to clip the back of her dress. *What's a few more seconds.* The hook wouldn't go through the loop. *Errr, who designs these things?*

Finally it went through. *Phew.* Poppy went back into her change room, but Suzy came out and asked me to zip up her dress. *Zip.*

I was about to leave when Ivy came out. "Can you help me with my buttons? Suzy can't even do up the first one."

I started at the bottom while Suzy kept fiddling with the top one. *I have to get out of here.* My heart raced but my fingers stiffened. I ended up doing all the buttons, said goodbye and slipped out of the store.

Running as fast as I could, I got to the dojo. Everyone on the mats stood in a straight line against the wall. I searched for Olive. She stood beside coding guy, and I waved, but she ignored me. The whole line bowed, and I realized I'd missed the whole thing.

Olive came off the mat. I went up to her. "Sorry I'm late."

"You're not late. You're *too* late." Her eyes zapped me like a laser before she grabbed her bag and disappeared into the change room.

I'll make it up to her.

CHAPTER 12

VISIBLE SPECTRUM

The part of the electromagnetic spectrum that is visible to the human eye.

It was the day of media presentations. Desks were pushed to the sides of the classroom and seats were placed in rows with a walkway through the centre. At the front was a table with a computer hooked up to a projector.

Olive turned away as soon as she saw me.

"I said I'm sorry."

She crossed her arms. "Actions speak louder than words."

I slowly raised my arm and jiggled my bracelet, hoping she wasn't too mad to clank it.

Just then, Poppy, Ivy and Suzy paraded in. Their hair and makeup were done up like they were going to the Oscars. Hair guy, breakdancing guy and head-bopper looked like they were about to topple over. Cole wasn't there yet.

Poppy and Suzy waved to me and I turned back to Olive. "Haven't you noticed we don't get made fun of anymore?"

"Speak for yourself." She glanced at them. "I think they're using you."

Momo Kesho immediately bounced into my head, but I ignored it. "I don't think so. They just didn't know us before, the way we know each other."

Godzilla snapped her fingers right between our faces. "We have a lot of presentations to get through." I tapped Olive on the shoulder to apologize again, but just as my mouth opened, Godzilla glared at me with her eyes of steel. Cole quietly came in and took a seat in the back corner.

Poppy, Ivy and Suzy were up first. Poppy handed me her phone and asked me to take pictures of her. Since Godzilla hated technology in class, I waited until she walked to the other side of the room.

Poppy removed her overcoat to reveal a red gown that made her look like a nominee for best actress. "Vancouver Fashion Week is underway . . ." She stepped forward in a pair of gold heels.

My mind was sucked suddenly into the past—an image of Mom dressed up with her favourite gold heels for Dad's company Christmas party. I shook my head and focused on the presentation.

"Over eighty local and international designers are here including CherryLea Thompson. She was only thirteen when she went to Paris to study under the one and only Mademoiselle LJ Robert." She said *Robert* with a French accent. "We have one of our correspondents in Paris right now for an interview with her. Over to you, Suzy."

Suzy tucked her jet-black hair behind her ears. She held a microphone to Ivy, who I assumed was the one and only Mademoiselle LJ Robert. "How was it being a mentor to the incredibly talented CherryLea Thompson?"

"Incroyable. She is a real génie," Ivy said with a convincing French accent. She wore a stylish blazer that suited her lengthy figure. Her designer sunglasses were so large, they covered half of her face.

My mind drifted. *What makes someone popular?* I doodled a list in my notebook.

"Pretty face"

"Nice hair"

"Stylish clothes"

"Symmetrical face"

I'd read that facial symmetry is associated with attractiveness. Using Poppy's phone on selfie mode, I looked at my own reflection, propping up my glasses and twisting my hair into a bun. *Pretty?* I studied my face from left to right.

My thoughts were interrupted when Godzilla cleared her throat. "How is this a misrepresentation of what is portrayed in the media?"

"Everyone thinks CherryLea Thompson is an adult," Ivy answered.

"But she's only a teenager," Suzy said. "The media makes her seem older than she is."

"Furthermore, the fashion industry is not as glamorous as it seems," Poppy added. "Being at the top is a lot of pressure. Everyone is always watching you."

That reminded me to take more pictures of Poppy. I slid her phone beside my desk to shield it from Godzilla's view before snapping a few shots. Poppy, Ivy and Suzy walked back to their seats, flashing smiles and waving their arms as if they were on the red carpet. Godzilla didn't look impressed.

Molly and Holly were next. They talked about how the media has led everyone to assume that twins have extrasensory perception. They explained that they couldn't always read each other's minds, but I could tell they were in sync.

When they finished, they joined hands and smiled like they were silently complimenting each other. I wished I had that person who understood me so well that I didn't always have this need to explain.

Next up were George and Cole. The usual giggles and sighs from girls swooning over Cole tickled the air. I didn't really pay much attention to what they were saying, but George looked nervous, not making eye contact and fiddling with his hands. Cole was a natural, which I guess wasn't surprising. He was good at making eye contact—so good in fact that he made me feel like I was the only one in the room.

Godzilla called our names and I started sweating like crazy. I should never have let Olive convince me to wear all black. I fluffed out my shirt to let in some air before stepping in front of the class.

Twenty-eight pairs of eyes zoomed in on me. "Hi, good morning. I mean . . . good afternoon." My voice quivered and the room fell silent.

"Emma!" exclaimed Godzilla. "We don't have all day." She crossed her arms and tapped her foot, making me more nervous.

Stretching out her arm, Olive gingerly tapped her bracelet with mine. I felt better but still couldn't speak. Olive took our homemade microphone out of my hand and began what I couldn't. "Good afternoon, everyone. We're here to talk about how girls are misrepresented in the media."

After giving the intro that I was supposed to do, she signalled me to start the slide show. Each slide was a picture of a girl or a group of girls our age in a magazine, product ad or show, looking glamorous and perfect.

The slide show ended with pictures of everyday girls. My nerves finally calmed and I was able to speak. "The girls in magazines, movies and marketing ads don't represent real life." I felt the class's undivided attention. "It puts a lot of unnecessary pressure on all of us to be flawless." I pointed to the last image of a real girl sitting on a park bench. "We should just be able to be ourselves."

I heaved a big sigh of relief as everyone including Poppy, Ivy and Suzy clapped. George grinned, so did Cole, and Molly and Holly nodded. But Godzilla just jotted down some notes.

After class, I thanked Olive for saving me.

"You would have done the same for me." I could tell by her voice that she hadn't fully forgiven me.

"I'm sorry I missed your practice."

"You've been a crappy friend."

"I know."

Her lips puckered. "But you're my *best* friend."

My shoulders relaxed. "Next time, I'll be there."

"It's too late for you to sign up now. Maybe I'll drop out."

"What? No."

"The whole point was to do something together."

"But you love it."

Olive's eyes lit up. "We did learn a cool move. I swear it's exactly the same one I saw in *Ninja Girls*."

"So stay."

Olive bit her bottom lip. "There's a demo this weekend. I'll stay in the club *only* if you come watch me."

"I promise." I crossed my heart.

She narrowed her eyes. "Remember, actions speak louder than words. I better get to practice." She smiled before trotting out.

Poppy strutted over in her long red gown and asked me

if I got any good photos of her. I handed back her phone. "This one's blurry . . . my eyes are closed . . . I still had my coat on in this one . . . oh this one's decent." She tapped her screen, uttering under her breath, "Media show. Wearing Bella Stella Bianchini. #glamour #redcarpet #reddress #goldheels." In the same low voice she asked, "Do you think it worked? Do you think Cole noticed me in this dress?"

I drew a blank. I didn't even have a chance to look over at Cole as I was too focused on her heels and my "popular" list.

"Books! We have to stay on track. Cole and I *have* to be on a holding-hands basis by the meet and greet, so everyone knows we're together."

"Umm . . . yeah, of course he noticed." I looked around while I thought of how to convince her. My eyes met Cole's, and he walked over with George, whose smile was as nervous as mine.

"Nice presentation!" Cole cocked his head.

"Yeah, great presentation, Poppy," added George. "I was just about to show Cole something. Come on."

Cole shrugged and waved goodbye to us before he followed George out the door.

Poppy grasped my arm. "Eek, he noticed." Then she gave me a funny look. "Books, you need a fashion makeover. Come over this weekend."

A huge smile flew onto my face.

WAVE MODEL

A depiction of light travelling as a wave.

As I walked through Garry Point on the way to Poppy's house, the sun shone with only a few popcorn-like clouds in the sky. I thought about my own cloud, which felt lighter these days, and a sense of joy washed over me.

I was surprised to see a stretch of snow on the field from one end of the park to the other. There was a gust of wind, and several snowflakes frolicked toward me. I crouched down to touch one, but it wasn't cold. It was fake.

From a distance I could see the *Magical Creatures* film crew preparing for a shoot. Several pixies pranced around on the fake snow with their shimmering wings.

I walked behind the park along the gravel trail lined with apartments and houses. Since I was coming to the back of her house, Poppy told me to watch out for an owl on the roof. "It's not real," she'd said, "but it's easy to spot."

Perched on a rooftop was a large white owl. Poppy's house was even bigger than I'd imagined. It had massive pillars, a window extending along three stories and a patio furnished with a fire pit, hot tub and barbecue.

A lady reclined on a chair reading a book with a sunset on its cover. When she saw me, she smiled and gently shook my hand with both of hers. "You must be Emma. I'm Poppy's mom." Something in her voice made me feel safe.

I followed her directions toward Poppy's room. All the walls and ceilings were stark white, but lush forest paintings, velvety pillows and large candles made the house feel cozy. A chandelier dangled like an acrobat from the high ceiling in the stairwell.

Poppy wasn't in the room that I felt certain was hers. Like the rest of the house, the room was spacious; unlike the rest of the house, it was a disaster. Clothes, shoes and accessories lay tossed everywhere. The only somewhat-organized piece of furniture was a bookshelf beside the bed. On the top shelf was a unicorn figurine and heart-shaped frame engraved with "Daddy's Girl." It held a picture of a younger Poppy and, presumably, her dad.

The rest of the shelves were filled with books. I recognized titles by Judy Blume, Grace Lin, Jacqueline Woodson and Susin Nielsen. As I skimmed them with my fingers, I heard laughter coming from behind a door.

Poppy, Ivy and Suzy were inside a closet the size of a fancy hotel elevator—full of clothes in every colour of the visible spectrum from red to violet. Scattered on the floor were more shoes than I'd ever owned in my whole entire life. Poppy motioned with her arm. "Come in, Books." I zoomed in on the gold heels that Poppy wore for her presentation, tangled on top of the dress she'd worn with it. An image erupted into my mind—Mom's favourite heels on top of her open suitcase.

"Books, try this on." Poppy handed me a knitted dress. Since I didn't have a bra like the others, I quickly pulled the dress over my clothes. A funny expression formed on their faces. I could feel my cheeks flush and excused myself to her en-suite bathroom.

I tried the dress again, this time without my layer of clothes. It was a little baggy in certain areas but other than that, it looked pretty good . . . at least that was what I thought.

Ivy and Suzy chuckled when I came out, and Poppy gave me another dress, which had a fitted top and a frilly bottom. As I headed to the bathroom, Poppy tossed me a thin-strapped tank top with a built-in bra. "Might look better with this on."

I put it on. Did it make me look better? I posed in the mirror but wasn't sure. I walked out anyway.

This time Poppy smiled and neither Ivy or Suzy said anything, which I took as a good sign. Poppy then pulled out a bunch of things from her closet: a few shirts, jeans, skirts and several tank tops. "Here, Books, you can have these. They're too small for me."

"Thanks!" I said as cool and calm as possible.

A song with a catchy beat came on, and the three of them leapt to their feet. "Let's make a TikTok video," said Poppy as she held up her phone to record Ivy and Suzy dancing. I copied them, but it was like I had two left feet and boneless arms. I stopped and stuffed my mouth with a handful of popcorn.

They watched the clip, laughing from their bellies. Just when I thought the embarrassment was over, they took turns taking pictures of themselves with puckered lips. Out of curiosity, I mimicked them but it felt funny and unnatural. Then they all tapped their phones like they were playing video games. *I hope they aren't posting any humiliating photos of me.*

One minute I felt good about myself and the next I felt like crap. Up and down . . . up and down, like light travelling in a wave. When Poppy suggested we do a quiz, I was relieved. Within seconds they were all back on their phones, searching for online quizzes. I picked up a teen magazine from the floor and flipped through it.

Not even a minute later, Ivy found one. "How old will you be when you get your first real boyfriend?" Poppy and

Suzy seemed eager, and I was just happy to be included.

Ivy read the first question.

1) How old are you?
    a. 9 and under
    b. 10–12
    c. 13–15
    d. 15 and over

Poppy, Ivy and Suzy were all thirteen, so they answered c. At twelve, I was a b.

"You're not even a teenager yet?" Ivy said in her usual condescending voice.

"My birthday isn't till the end of the year," I said. *I can't help it.*

Poppy read the next question.

2) Do you have a crush?
    a. Yes, I have many.
    b. Yes, I have one.
    c. Does a celebrity count?
    d. No.

Ivy gave a half-suppressed laugh. "I've got many."

"Hugh Gilmore from the show *Sweet Fraser High* is so cute!" Suzy fanned herself. "c, does a celebrity count?"

"Hmm, I'm kinda b and c. I have a crush who happens to be a celebrity." Poppy let out a long sigh.

"What's wrong?" asked Suzy.

"So many girls like him already," she answered. "And he's only gaining more fans, not less."

"I don't get it," said Suzy.

"Isn't it obvious?" Ivy interrupted. "Poppy has to stake a claim for Cole before someone else does."

"Not exactly," said Poppy. "But since the winner gets a face-to-face with him, there's a chance he could end up liking that person. If Cole and I aren't a thing by the meet and greet, it's all over."

A heavy weight dropped on my shoulders.

"Why don't you just ask him out?" said Suzy.

Ivy's eyes narrowed. "'Cause she doesn't want to seem desperate. Duh!"

Suzy bit her lip as Poppy twirled her hair. "At least my chances for winning the contest are better than anyone else's." She winked at me.

I smiled back but suddenly my face tensed. My chances were doubled since I'd also entered for Olive. *I can't win. Who would I pick?* Choosing the wrong person would be like adding the wrong reagent to a chemical reaction— everything could blow up in my face. My palms started to sweat and my eyes flickered everywhere. They landed on Poppy's unicorn figurine. It reminded me of Holly and Molly dressed as a unicorn. Wait . . . if it was purely based on statistics, Molly and Holly would win. They'd entered at least three times each with different costumes, and there were two of them. *No need to panic.* I rubbed the sweat off my palms and answered. "d, I don't have a crush."

"You don't like anyone?" Poppy asked. "What about George?"

"What about George?"

She gave me a knowing look. "He has a thing for you. He's always nervous around you."

Good thing she has no idea he's my catalyst. "No I don't think so. Next question," I said.

3) Which fruit do your breasts most resemble?
    a. Grapes (training bra)
    b. Plums (A-AA)
    c. Apples (B-C)
    d. Melons (D+)

Hmm, here I thought mine were like raisins. Then Ivy piped up. "Emma's are more like raisins." Suzy laughed even though she wasn't far ahead. Poppy and Ivy were no bigger than fist-sized apples, but Ivy pushed out her chest and answered, "d, melons," then quickly moved onto the next question.

4) Do you have any hair on your legs or armpits?
    a. None.
    b. Some—I can count them.
    c. More than I can count, but they are light.
    d. So many that I have to shave.

"I've been shaving like forever," Ivy gloated, and I didn't get why. But then again we were never on the same wavelength.

Suzy lifted up her arm and looked under it. She looked disappointed that she had none.

Poppy said, "I have more than I can count, but they're so light I don't need to shave." They all stared at my legs. I had none.

How was any of this related to getting a boyfriend?

Then the dreaded question.

5) When did you get your first period?
    a. 9 or under
    b. 10–11
    c. 12–13
    d. 14+

Just talking about it made me light-headed. Ivy said she got hers when she was ten. Poppy was twelve, and Suzy said she was sure she was getting hers soon. Again all eyes were on me. Again I had no idea how any of this had anything to do with getting a boyfriend.

6) Do you wear deodorant?
    a. No, I don't have to.
    b. I should, but I don't.
    c. When I exercise.
    d. Yes, every day.

"Yes, every day," Ivy bragged.

"c, when I exercise," answered Suzy.

Ivy turned to Suzy. "You should have answered b, not c." Suzy did a side sniff of her underarm.

Poppy shrugged. "I don't think I need to wear any."

"Me neither," I said. I didn't mind this question or the next.

7) Do you have pimples?

   a. None

   b. A couple

   c. A few

   d. Several or more

"I have none," I said. Ivy and Suzy glared at me like they did at the start of the school year. "b," said Ivy, but with a sheepish grin. Her face was coated with cover-up makeup. Suzy rested her palm on the one zit she had on her chin. It was clear that Poppy had the most flawless skin.

8) Do you care about what boys think of you?

   a. No

   b. Kind of

   c. Sometimes

   d. Always

"I don't really care." Ivy flicked her hair. "If guys don't like me, they're missing out."

Suzy shrugged. "I'm somewhere in between b and c."

"I hate to admit it, but yes I do," said Poppy.

I answered no and got the glares again.

9) Do you consider yourself pretty?

   a. No

   b. Sometimes

   c. Often

   d. Always

Ivy flaunted her figure. "Absolutely."

Suzy answered with, "I'm leaning toward c."

"b," said Poppy. Ivy and Suzy looked as shocked as I was. I thought b for myself. How could Poppy see herself the way I saw myself? It made no sense. But neither did this quiz.

Ivy tallied up the points and shared the results. "I was ready for a boyfriend like a year ago. Poppy, you're pretty much ready; Suze, you're not ready for another year; and Emma, you're light years away."

"Speaking of pretty, is your mom home yet?" Poppy asked.

My heart jolted.

"Did you get our samples?" Ivy said.

I exhaled a shaky breath. "Right, the makeup."

All three of them raised their plucked eyebrows. In a nervous babble, words tumbled out of my mouth. "Research shows that skimping on sleep can lead to increased levels of inflammation and stress hormones, which can exacerbate skin problems like acne."

Ivy drilled her eyes into me. "I told you I don't get much sleep 'cause of my baby sister. Stop stressing me out!"

I gritted my teeth.

"When is she back, Books?" asked Poppy.

I thought back to the last thing Mom said to me: "See you soon, Emma."

"Soon." I only realized what I had said after the words came out. Mom still hadn't returned my calls, and it had been a while since I spoke to her. She must be busy working . . . travelling. *That's it!* She probably just travelled to a place with no signal. "She's somewhere remote, where the reception's poor. She's in a small mountainous village." *Why can't I just stop?*

"I thought she was in Paris," said Poppy.

Gulp. "She was, but she's already moved on. Just part of the film biz, I guess."

"Wow, the freedom you must have. I wish my mom would leave like that," Suzy huffed.

Ivy pressed her lips together. "A check-in would be nice once in a while." She looked at me with her eyes somewhat sincere for once. "So when is she home?"

I looked down at my watch and read two o'clock. "In two days," I said.

The interrogation stopped.

At least for the time being.

SECOND LAW of THERMODYNAMICS

Entropy or disorder of the universe will increase over time.

Two days? Why didn't I give myself more time? How was I going to get makeup samples that didn't exist? My mind spun like a cyclone.

I went to Mom's room to see if I could find anything. As usual, Dad's side was messy and Mom's was tidy, especially around her antique vanity embossed with metal vines and roses. It was so clean that it looked untouched, like it was part of a showroom display. Searching through her drawers, I found some lipstick, eyeshadow and foundation. Unfortunately they were all used.

In the bottom drawer was a bottle of perfume, which I spritzed above me. The scent stirred up a memory of Dad making a custom fragrance for Mom, steam distilling her favourite flowers. This gave me an idea, and I made my way down the stairs.

The comforting smell of steamed rice, green tea and soup wafted toward me. The clinks and clanks of glassware made my heart beat with excitement. I imagined Dad back to performing his kitchen experiments, infusing flavours in his test tubes, pouring a liquid into a volumetric flask and swirling it around as it changed colours.

The kitchen was messy but Dad wasn't cooking. He was eating *ochazuke*, a quick-fix meal made by adding a packet of dried ingredients and hot water to a bowl of leftover rice: as simple as making a cup of instant noodles.

I sighed. He slurped. It was still worth a shot. "Hey, Dad, do you think you could help me make some makeup?"

He peered up from his bowl. "You're too young for makeup."

"It's not for me."

"Then what's it for?"

If I tell him it's for a friend, his answer's going to be the same. "It's for a school project."

"You have all the tools you need," he tapped his temple, "up here."

"I thought it would be fun to do something together, like we used to." After the words came out, I realized it wasn't just about the makeup. I really missed the way we used to be. From the look in his eyes, I thought for sure he would agree. "We could make some extra for Mom. Maybe she could try it out on her clients."

He got up abruptly. "I have work to finish."

"Fine then, I'll do it myself." I just didn't know how.

The phone rang and it was Olive. "Guess what?" She didn't wait for an answer. "The meet and greet is going to have Wentworth the Wizard performing magic *and* Empress Octavia showing off her signature move."

"Does that mean there's an audience? Why don't you just get a ticket for the show?"

"I already got one, but it's not the same thing."

"What do you mean?"

"Would you rather watch Einstein perform an experiment *right* in front of you or watch from the sidelines?"

"I guess the closer the better."

"That's why one of us has to win!"

"When's the winner chosen?"

"Halloween."

"That's only a few more weeks."

"I guess." Her voice perked up. "Remember the demo tonight."

"How could I forget, Olive."

I went back to my room and looked around for more makeup ideas. My experimental plants were still wilting, but they looked like they had a chance, so I gave them some more water and homemade fertilizer.

Below them sat my bunny bank. I quickly dumped it out and counted how much money I had. It wasn't quite enough to buy name-brand makeup, but as I put the coins back into the bunny, an idea hopped into my mind.

I dumped all the money into my wallet, slipped on a scoop neck shirt from Poppy and headed to the Japanese dollar store where Dad had bought my bunny bank. They carried everything from home and garden accessories to stationery and snacks imported from Japan.

When I got there, I made a beeline for the huge cosmetics section. Shelves on top of shelves lined a wall with every-thing from lip stuff and blush to eye makeup and false lashes. I filled my basket with as much as my wallet could afford: three lipsticks, three blushes and some foundation, all with a peach tint. With the money left over, I bought some peach-coloured cellophane and chocolate Pocky sticks.

On the bus ride home I mulled over how to design the label for the so-called Momo Kesho brand. I pulled out my notepad and doodled until I ended up with several swirls, each with a peach on top—except the peach didn't look like a peach. I ripped out the sheet of paper and started over, trying several more times, each with no success. *Ugh!*

Before I knew it, my bag became a recycling bin of scrunched up paper. I stopped and stared at the word *MoMo*, but the only thing that came to mind was two symbols of molybdenum, *Mo*, next to each other. What did I expect? *I'm not artsy.* I blamed my science mind for hijacking my brain and gave up.

I fished out an issue of *Science Today and Tomorrow* and read about the second law of thermodynamics: how disorder is always favoured in the universe. It was true— it's always easier to make a mess than to clean it up.

After getting off the bus I didn't feel like going home, so I walked around Garry Point where the *Magical Creatures* crew was out again. Film and lighting equipment crowded the beach, and a majestic tall ship sailed in the background.

"Hey!" I turned around to see a guy wearing a cloak with an amulet around his neck. When he removed his hood, I saw that it was Cole. "What are you up to?" he asked.

I wasn't about to go into detail. "Just getting a breath of fresh air." Wait, this was my chance to learn more about Cole. "What's your favourite movie?"

"*Magical Creatures.*"

"What's your favourite food?"

"Pizza."

"Of course." He was in that stretchy cheese commercial. "Favourite colour?"

"Sunset orange." Go figure, the same colour as *Stretcheeeeesy.* "Favourite drink?"

"Chamomile tea."

"Really?" I snickered. "Out of all beverages?"

"What? It's calming."

"It contains antioxidants which have been shown to help with diabetes and cancer, but the research is preliminary and therefore inconclusive."

He smirked. "You're different."

"What do you mean?"

"You treat me like I'm just a guy."

"You *are* just a guy." The wind blew hair in my face.

He moved my bangs out of my eyes, skimming his fingers across my forehead. I felt a strange tickle up my spine. It was probably the wind ruffling the shirt on my back.

"I like how you take the time to know me." His deep green eyes locked with mine.

"Why wouldn't I?"

"Most people assume they know me already. They come up to me and say they love me, but only because I'm in some TV show or commercial."

"Would you rather they not love you?"

"Don't get me wrong. Of course I feel lucky to be part of this show, but I wish people would like me for who I am. It's hard to get any realness, if you know what I mean."

"I think a little unrealness is nice once in a while."

Cole tilted his head like he was thinking.

"You're an actor . . . isn't it refreshing sometimes to pretend to be someone you're not? An escape from reality."

"Maybe, but you eventually have to come back to the real world."

"I guess."

He swept his arm along the landscape. "What would you be if you could be anything out there?"

"Hmm." I looked around and pointed to the tall ship. "That! It's so grand and beautiful." Then I stretched up. "And it'd be nice to be tall for a change."

He chuckled.

"What?" I crossed my arms. "I'm not joking. People constantly bump into me like I don't exist. I have to work extra hard to prove myself, and I need a step stool to reach up high. Not to mention, research shows that height matters when it comes to success. Taller people fare better."

Cole admitted he didn't see it that way. "I always thought short people had it easier. They have more leg room in cars and airplanes, they're good at hide-and-seek *and* it's easier for them to slip through a crowd." He gazed outward.

"What would you be?" I asked him.

"I'd be a ripple in the water, blending in with my surroundings and relaxing to the sound of the waves."

"That's deep . . . for an eighth grader."

"I'm actually a year older. I fell behind in a few classes." His cheeks flushed.

"Oh so that's why you're taller." I stood on my tippy-toes and caught a glimpse of his dimples. I was beginning to see why girls thought he was cute.

A lady with a headset waved him over. "Why don't you stay and watch?" he asked.

I thought about having to package all the makeup samples and still come up with a believable logo. "Sorry, I can't."

"We'll be here for the next few hours if you change your mind."

"Sounds good." Before I left, I needed to know one last thing. "So what do you think of Poppy?"

"Who?" His eyebrows formed an upside-down V shape.

"You know, the girl whose shoe you caught . . . the girl with me at the signing . . . the one wearing the red dress." *Oh boy, this is not good.* "Poppy Sinclair?"

"Oh yeah, I think I know who you're talking about."

You think? My arms jetted out. "You told her you liked her presentation. I was there."

"I was talking to you, Emma. It's interesting what you said about the media putting a lot of unnecessary pressure on . . ."

What? "You weren't talking to Poppy?" *What a disaster.*

As soon as Cole went back to set, I rushed to George's house to get some answers.

CHAPTER 15

BOILING POINT

The temperature at which point a liquid becomes a vapour.

When George opened the door, I didn't even give him a chance to talk. "Cole barely knows who Poppy is. What gives?"

He rubbed his palms together. "I told you to give it time. Be patient."

"Poppy's going to be *so* disappointed. We have to do something!"

He narrowed his eyes and nodded, like he was plotting something. "What does she like?"

"Why do you care?"

"No reason." He turned away. "Just thought if I knew more about her, it could help with the advice I'm giving you."

I guess that makes sense. "She likes books." Then I lifted up my bag. "And she also likes makeup. But . . ."

"But what?"

"I'm supposed to give her these makeup samples, but I told her they were from some fancy international cosmetics company, which they're not." I opened the bag to show him the knock-offs. "I don't have the time or the talent to transform them into something more." I heaved a huge *fail* sigh.

George's hand slid along his chin. "These makeup samples . . . they'd make Poppy happy?"

I nodded.

In a flash, he brought out his tablet. "What's the company called?"

I unravelled a scrunched-up paper from my bag to show him one of my many attempts at drawing the company logo. "*Momo* stands for peach, and *Kesho* means makeup."

He focused on the screen and his fingers glided, tapped and swirled. A few minutes later he turned the screen toward me. Displayed was the prettiest peach I'd ever seen. It was enveloped in a luminescent swirl like it was floating, and *MoMo Kesho* was written above in an arc shape.

"Wow, George, that looks great!"

He ran his hand through his hair. "Do you think Poppy will like it?"

"Yes, but now I have to wrap the makeup to make it look professional." I stuck out my tongue.

"I could do it."

Why? He probably felt bad that his advice hadn't been working. I wasn't about to refuse his offer.

He took the bag of makeup with the peach cellophane. "Don't worry. Poppy will get the attention she wants."

I smiled, relieved. Everything was working out.

On my way home from George's, I passed Poppy's place and remembered that Cole was still filming. When I rang her doorbell, she opened the door in sweats, holding a book with a girl riding a dragon on the cover.

"Hey, Poppy, sorry I didn't call . . . you know I don't have a phone. Anyway, Cole's at Garry Point shooting a scene."

She put down her book. "Right now?" Before I could say another word, she sprinted upstairs. Within a few minutes she was back down in a pair of jeans, a shirt with sleeves up to her fingertips and her hair in a high ponytail.

Trailers wrapped around the park, and the scene was action packed. Goblins and trolls scrambled along the beach. Guys in cloaks, one of them Cole, circled Wentworth the Wizard, who boarded the tall ship. Even though we were watching from a distance, excitement filled the air.

Poppy was spellbound. "Cole's so cute. Be honest, Books. What are the chances we'll be a couple before the meet and greet?"

"Er . . . I heard there will be some performances there.

Why don't we get tickets for the audience, just in case you don't win the contest."

"Are you kidding?" Poppy looked at me as if I was out of my mind. "Would you rather be on stage, hand-holding distance from your crush, or watch from a distance as someone else cozies up to him? Not to mention that all eyes will be on the winner."

"I guess the closer the better." I hastily pointed to the tall ship. "Wouldn't it be cool to board one of those?" She looked up, and I was thankful her attention was back on the film shoot.

The director kept shouting, "Cut . . . Action . . . Cut . . ." re-shooting the scene over and over. Cole kept adjusting the hood on his cloak.

All of a sudden Poppy gave me a side hug. "Thanks for coming to get me. This is amazing!" She took out her phone, put her arm around my shoulder and snapped a selfie of the two of us before tapping her phone. "Having a blast with Books."

She mentioned me. I was more excited than an energized electron.

"So how did you know Cole was filming here today?" she asked.

I looked over at the makeup trailer, and I imagined Mom inside, transforming ordinary faces into something extraordinary. "My mom told me about it."

"When can I meet her?"

"Umm . . . she went away again . . . on business."

"So she was home? Did you get the makeup samples?"

If George wrapped the makeup half as well as he designed the logo, I knew I had nothing to worry about. "I did."

When the sun was on the brink of setting, the film crew started wrapping up. From afar I heard laughter from a group of people all dressed in black. At first I thought they were part of the show, but looking closer I realized they weren't.

"We missed it," said a guy in the group.

"They're supposed to be filming here for the next few days," said someone else who I recognized as coding guy.

"Let's come back," said another familiar voice.

Olive. Her demo. I skittered behind Poppy.

"What are you doing, Books?"

Olive caught sight of me, so I ran up to her. "It's not what you're thinking . . ."

"What am I thinking?" Her words bubbled with anger.

"I had this chance to watch the filming of . . . I know how much you love *Magical Creatures*. I knew you were busy . . . thought you'd be more mad if I didn't stay and watch. I swear I was going to give you an update." Olive's eyes crawled toward Poppy, who was taking photos. "Poppy even came with me to take pictures . . . so I could show you."

By the look on her face, she didn't care. "You promised."

"I'm sorry, Olive."

"How could you do this to me? I've *always* been there for you. Why can't you be there for me?" She shifted her gaze back toward Poppy. "All this time I thought you were just going through something. Clearly I'm not important to you anymore." Her eyes welled up.

"You are." I swallowed a lump. "I'm really sorry."

"You said that already." She whipped around and walked off, leaving the air damp with sorrow.

All I could hear in my mind was "actions speak louder than words."

THE THEORY OF PLATE TECTONICS

The movements of the plates that make up the Earth's outer shell.

In science the next day, I headed straight to Olive to apologize again. As soon as she saw me, she turned her back and said something to Molly and Holly. They opened up a seat for her, and she sat between them. My shoulders slumped when I noticed she wasn't wearing her DNA bracelet. "Did you hear that the meet and greet is going to be filmed live at the VTVZ studio?" She sounded totally fine, which made me more upset.

As I thought of a way to make it up to Olive, Poppy came in and looped her arm around mine. Ivy and Suzy were close behind her, and they all asked me about the makeup samples. "Soon," I said and searched for George, who came in with Cole. I waved my arm to get George's attention, but Cole must have thought it was for him because he walked toward me.

Poppy grasped my arm and widened her eyes. "Books, quick, trade places with me."

So I did. Poppy fluttered her eyelashes like butterfly wings. Cole took a seat beside her, and I saw her smile blossom.

All of a sudden we heard a really loud blare. Mr Timberlac entered the classroom with his entire body trembling as though the earth beneath him shook. "Attention, class, duck under your tables and cover your heads."

A couple of girls near Cole squeezed in under the same desk as him. Poppy was so busy fixing her hair that she missed her chance. Breakdancing guy and hair guy slipped below a desk near Poppy, but she ended up coming under the same table as me. George joined us soon after. Poppy elbowed me and whispered in my ear, "See I told you George likes you."

I played along and winked at George as he stared in our direction. He legitimately looked nervous, like there was an actual earthquake.

Mr Timberlac stopped the alarm. "Earth is a dynamic planet." He pulled out a globe to show the major tectonic plates. "The outer layer is made up of rigid plates that move with respect to one another. The most destructive natural disasters occur at the tectonic plate boundaries. For example . . ." He slid two plates past each other and stopped. "If these get stuck, energy builds up. When they detach, the energy released can be so powerful that it can cause the Earth to shake." He trembled out the door.

Ivy snickered. "Like when Olive walks."

"Yeah." Suzy joined in.

Normally, Olive had a comeback, but she didn't say anything. She just looked down with her back hunched over, and I was mad at myself for not saying something to defend her.

Mr Timberlac jumped back in and made an announce-ment. "We're having a big test next week, one that covers everything from the beginning of term." He started shak-ing once again and shaped his hands like a funnel over his mouth. "The BIG one's coming. Get it?" He snorted while laughing. He reminded us that the test would be a mix of topics in no particular order. "The sooner you learn to in-tegrate everything, the better off you'll be."

After class a few girls ran up to Cole, and I heard him say he was in a rush. As he left, his eyes met mine and he gave me a nod.

I turned to George. "Do you have the makeup?" From the corner of my eye, I noticed Poppy still in her seat with a frown on her face. I went up to her and George followed me.

"What's wrong?" I asked.

"I'm so behind. I've been so focused on social media and trying to get Cole to notice me, I totally haven't been paying attention. And I've barely touched my assignments." She flopped her head back. "Just because I'm popular doesn't mean I don't care about my grades."

She caught me by surprise. "I can help you study." This was something I could actually help her with.

"You could!" Then her expression fell, and she asked George if she could have a minute with me. As soon as he stepped away, she said, "I'm pretty sure Cole's not into me. I said hi to him. He said hi back, but it was really impersonal. Like I was a stranger." Her voice raised. "Are you sure you know what you're doing?"

I needed to talk to George. Then I remembered that he had the makeup samples. "I'll be right back."

I leaned into George and whispered, "Poppy's getting suspicious. We need to do something."

He looked over at her. "When you go over to her place to study, I'll come too!"

"What? Why?"

"It's time to shake things up! I'll bring Cole with me."

Poppy looked straight at us, so I didn't have time to ask him more questions. When I walked back to her with the makeup samples, her eyes lit up. "George is so sweet." *Huh?* "Him carrying the makeup for you." She gazed up. "I wish I had a guy as nice as him."

A nervous laugh crept out of my throat.

Poppy pulled out her phone and took pictures of the makeup. "Unique . . . made in Japan . . . ooh peach emoji."

While Poppy was busy on her phone, tapping her screen, I pulled out my C Ho Co La Te notebook and made some notes: *"The Earth's outer layer is composed of plates that shift. Sometimes they stick together."* I pretty much summarized what Mr Timberlac said. *"When they separate, energy is released, which causes the ground to shake."* I thought about Poppy and Cole as two plates. *"Advice four: If things are not moving along with a guy and you feel stuck, you need to do something to shake things up!"*

Since I had no idea what George was planning, I decided to hold on to this advice until I went to Poppy's.

SUBDUCTION

A geological process in which the edge of one plate descends below the edge of another.

I packed up my flashcards and study notes and headed to Poppy's. On the way it started to drizzle. Within seconds the raindrops were the size of gumdrops, and I was soaking wet.

Poppy's mom opened the door, and her eyes nearly popped. "You should've called me. I could have picked you up."

"That's okay, I don't mind a little rain." I dried my glasses on my shirt as the smell of something freshly baked drifted toward me.

Poppy's mom brought a towel and helped me take off my jacket before offering me some tea. I followed her to the kitchen while admiring the floating lights in the foyer. *How's that physically possible?* Something had to be holding them up. I studied them as we walked and saw that there were super slim strings between the lights and ceiling.

The kitchen was bright and welcoming, with a large island in the centre. The pendant lights above shone onto a

pan of chocolate chip cookies. She placed one on a plate and gave it to me along with a cup of tea. The cookie was warm and so moist that it practically melted in my mouth.

"How's school, Emma?" Such a simple question and yet it meant so much.

"I'm really enjoying science."

"Poppy mentioned that your dad is a scientist."

"He's a chemist," I answered then quickly changed the subject. "What do you do, Mrs Sinclair?"

"I'm an interior designer." She pointed up and spun her finger around. "I designed this place."

"That's so cool. I really like it here."

"Well thank you. You're welcome here anytime." I felt a strange feeling in my chest, like my heart was wrapped in a blanket.

Before I had another thought, Poppy came in and we went downstairs to the game room to study. "Science is by far my most difficult subject." She complained that Mr Timberlac's notes were all over the place, kind of like him. "Why does he have to teach everything out of order?"

"Like he said, science is everywhere. I think he just wants to challenge us to think out of the box. These should help." I pulled out my flashcards and read a question:

What are the types of plate tectonic movements?
    a. convergent
    b. divergent
    c. transform
    d. all of the above

Poppy stared at the ceiling. "Why does Cole have to be so irresistible?"

"The answer is d, all of the above." It was obvious she wasn't paying any attention to me. Since George was going to be here any minute, and Cole was the only thing on her mind, I handed her my science of boys notes.

"Shake things up? What does that even mean?"

"One more flashcard, and I'll tell you more about it." I kept glancing at the sliding door.

Ivy and Suzy strutted down the stairs. "Why weren't we invited to the party?" Ivy's face scrunched up like she'd eaten a bitter lime.

Poppy asked them the same question I was wondering about, "What are you doing here?"

"We saw your post," Suzy answered. "About the makeup."

As soon as I handed them their samples, Ivy ripped hers open. She immediately applied the foundation to her face.

She turned toward me, and I thought for sure she was going to complain. Instead she said, "Not bad," and continued to pat her nose.

I was surprised to see Suzy grab my flashcards in favour of the makeup. "What are these?"

"Study cards," I answered.

"Can I join?" she asked. "My parents are threatening to take away my phone if my grades don't improve."

"Sure." I was happy somebody was interested. Just as I was about to read the next flashcard, Poppy pressed me more about my latest advice. I looked at my watch then at the sliding door. It was time but George wasn't here. *Keep stalling.* "I thought we agreed to go over one more flashcard." I read the next question before she could say anything else.

What is subduction?
    a. when two plates move away from each other
    b. when two plates touch
    c. when the plates crumble
    d. when one plate slides underneath another plate

Poppy's eyes wandered and Suzy's eyebrows knitted together. Realizing they weren't going to answer, I said, "It's d, when a plate slides underneath another."

From the other side of the room, Ivy hollered, "Just *slide* the answers underneath our papers?" A wicked smile formed on her face.

Poppy's eyes opened wide. "Would you do that?"

"Umm . . ." I kept looking at the sliding door. *George, any time now!*

Suzy fiddled with her sleeve. "My parents praise my brothers and sisters all the time, but never me." Then she gazed up at me. "Doing well on this test could change things."

I looked at my watch again. George was late.

"Books!" Poppy squeezed her palms together. "Pleeease."

George and Cole aren't coming . . . I crumbled. "Okay, I'll do it—I'll help you on the test."

Moments later there was a tap on the door. George was finally here with Cole. Poppy sprang up, immediately fixed her hair and put on some lip gloss.

The sliding door opened and George and Cole came in. George handed Poppy a book with a picture of an eye and a makeup brush. I thought this was a bit strange, but then she passed the book to me. "He's so sweet, Books. He got you a book about makeup."

George kept looking at me and then at Poppy. She followed Cole, who said, "George told me you were going to be here."

"Of course I'd be here. I live here." She giggled with hearts in her eyes. Cole's eyes converged with mine, and he gave me a confused look, so I shrugged and elbowed George. He pulled out a video game with tennis rackets on it. "Two against two?"

Right away, Poppy said, "Cole and I will be one team." Ivy was still puttering around with the makeup, and Suzy was flipping through the flashcards.

George and I teamed up and we played several matches. Every time the ball went up high, Poppy jumped up as if she were on court. Every time someone served, a swoosh blared. Whenever Poppy and Cole won a point, they'd high-five each other, and she'd give me a wide-eyed grin.

George seemed ultra-competitive and kept glaring at them. At one point he was so focused on them that his character rammed right into the net. The sounds from the game bellowed. *Wham, oops.* He did this several times. *Wham, oops . . . wham, oops.* The final time he did it, he fell over the net and collapsed onto the ground. *Crash!* We laughed hysterically.

All of a sudden we heard, "What's all the commotion down there?" *Poppy's mom.*

George and Cole darted toward the door while George quickly glanced at Poppy and then at Cole. He was wondering the same thing I was: did they hit it off?

Poppy's mom came downstairs with some milk and cookies. "How's the studying coming along? What was all that noise?"

"Books just showed us the effects of two tectonic plates crashing into each other." Poppy smashed her hands together. *"Bang!"* she said, cracking a smile.

As soon as her mom went upstairs, Poppy became giddy. "How did you get the guys to come over?"

"You know Cole is George's cousin and . . ."

Poppy's arms shot up. "You and George . . . you're a thing now?"

"Um . . ." I bit my tongue. Maybe it was okay to let Poppy think that George and I were a thing. This was my chance to bond with her, confiding in each other, sharing secrets and talking about our crushes. I didn't want to lose that.

Stay calm. Act cool. "I mean . . . kinda. But I don't want to make a big deal out of it."

Poppy made a toast. "To new relationships." I didn't know if she was referring to our friendship, mine and George's fake relationship or to the new one that was about to form between her and Cole. But it didn't matter. She was happy and we clinked cups. I was so caught up in the moment, I accidentally took a sip of milk. My stomach instantly churned.

I excused myself to the washroom. Luckily I'd only taken a sip. When I came out, Poppy put her arm around me. "Maybe we could all hang out? You and George with me and Cole."

My mind drifted as I pictured the four of us together. It wasn't that far-fetched. We did just play a fun game of tennis together.

A grumble sounded, but it wasn't coming from my tummy. Ivy and Suzy gave me razor-edged stares, and my blissful bubble popped.

EMuLSIFICATION

The combination of two substances that typically do not mix well together.

How was I going to help Poppy, Ivy and Suzy cheat on this test? Yet another promise I didn't know if I could keep. I went to the kitchen to look for some chocolate.

Dad was drinking orange juice in his beaker mug. This was the first time I saw him touch his chemistry kitchenware since I'd pulled it out, and it made me hopeful that he was becoming his old self again.

"Hey, Dad, say you had a friend who wanted your help with something."

"Then I'd help them." He poured maple syrup into a volumetric flask.

"What if the help they wanted meant that you had to do something you knew was wrong?"

"Then I wouldn't do it." As he placed the cap back on, his hand knocked over the flask, and syrup guzzled out. "Oh buckyballs." He walked to the sink, and I saw a sock clinging to the back of his corduroy pants. Maybe he wasn't the best person to ask for social advice.

After he sat back down, I asked him what he was reading.

"Tips for emulsification—how to mix a hydrophobic compound with a hydrophilic compound, like oil and water." Then he looked right at me. "How did that school project go?"

Why is he asking me about school all of a sudden? Did he know I was about to cheat?

"This article may help. Emulsification is often used in the cosmetics industry."

A sigh of relief came out. "Thanks. I've got that under control." I gave him a thumbs up and jetted off before he picked up on anything.

I walked around Garry Point, contemplating. *To cheat or not to cheat?* My thoughts were interrupted by a unicorn galloping past in the distance. It had a rainbow mane, sparkly wings and a crown around the horn. By the time I got closer, the film crew had started removing the costume and accessories. What was left was an ordinary horse.

Not wanting to go home, I went to Maritime Anytime. I grabbed a soy hot chocolate, a science journal with what looked like proteins growing out of a pot on the cover and a comfy seat in the corner of the café. I barely got past the abstract of the featured article when the bell clanged and Poppy walked in.

This was my chance to convince her that she still had time to study. Before I could say a word, she let out a deep breath. "My dad's been working on a big project and hasn't been home for a while. I miss him." Then she looked around. "I know it sounds silly but being surrounded by these books reminds me of him."

Now I really appreciated my nickname. I told her it

didn't sound silly at all. I wanted to tell her I felt the same whenever I was near anything that reminded me of Mom. But I said nothing.

Up until now I had thought Poppy and I were like oil and water, different as could be. The more I got to know her, the more I realized we had things in common.

Neither of us said anything for a while. It was nice to just sit around with her and read, me with a chemistry magazine and Poppy with a book that had a jellyfish on the cover.

After a while she asked me what I was reading. I lifted up the journal to show her the cover. "I'm reading about artificial proteins."

Her eyebrows raised but her eyes were sincere. "Have you always wanted to be a scientist?"

"Ever since I was five," I said. "My dad constantly asked me questions that made me wonder why things happen and how things work. What do you want to be?"

"I'd love to be a writer." She pointed at the shelves. "Maybe even have my books here one day."

"That's great!" I told her. "What's your favourite book of all time?"

"*Are You There God? It's Me, Margaret*, by Judy Blume. Have you seen the redesigned cover?" She pulled it up on her phone, a picture with a text message to God. I didn't know what to think of it, but she went on to say how clever she thought it was.

Poppy's phone dinged and she hastily tapped her screen. "Oh darn, how did I miss that?" After a few more taps and swipes, she suddenly leapt up and shrieked. "Cole's following me!" She showed me her screen. "Books, you were right again. I needed to be patient." Then she looked at her phone again. "Now I have more followers."

"Why do you care so much about how many followers you have?"

"Books." She looked at me like I was the crazy one. "You need tens of thousands of followers to become an influencer."

"I thought you wanted to be a writer?"

"I do, but do you know how hard it is to become a full-time author? To make a living out of it?"

I shrugged. I had never thought about it.

"Either way, it's important to build a network." Her eyes were glued to her screen. Her fingers slid and tapped.

If this were Olive I'd tell her that I thought this whole thing was silly, trying to get approval from people she didn't even know. But for some reason I couldn't with Poppy. I just told her I thought it was a cool backup idea.

I went back to the journals to choose another one to read. Then I saw an article about volcanic eruptions, and it reminded me of the upcoming science test.

Poppy and I were getting along. Maybe she'd see where I was coming from, so I just went for it. "There's still time to study for the test."

She peered up from her screen, nose crinkled. Her phone dinged, and she typed something before gazing back in my direction. "I just need to pull up my grades. Just this once, okay?"

I didn't know what else to say.

Later that day I called Mom again. *She'd know what to do. She has a lot of friends.* As I waited for her to pick up, I started imagining what she would say. "Friends are important, Emma. Be good to them." Although she never answered her phone, I felt better knowing Mom would be on my side.

LAW OF CONSERVATION OF MASS

In a closed system, mass is neither created nor destroyed.

The morning of the big science test arrived. A lump sat in my throat while I waited in the hallway for Mr Timberlac to prepare the classroom.

I pulled out an issue of *Science Today and Tomorrow* and read about how to test the law of conservation of mass using microwave popcorn. The question: "Does the bag's mass change or stay the same after the popcorn has popped?"

Normally I'd be all over it, answering the question and explaining why the mass stays the same. But I couldn't focus. All I could think was that I was about to become a co-conspirator in a cheating scam. The lump in my throat made its way down and became a knot in my shoulder.

Suzy walked over and, squeezing my arm, said, "Thanks for helping me. My youngest brother skipped a grade. If I fail, we could end up in the same class next year. That *can't* happen." She walked away, cracking her fingers. I shrugged my shoulders several times, but the weight on them would not go away.

The bell rang and I plodded into the classroom, where the exams lay face down on each desk.

Mr Timberlac wore a black-and-white referee outfit. "Class, turn your papers over and begin." He blew a whistle then ran around the classroom like he was actually reffing a game, waving his arms and pivoting every time he turned.

I flipped the paper over and surveyed the test. Mostly multiple choice with a few open-ended questions. For a moment I was fine—this was like any other test.

Then I felt a kick on my chair. I turned around to see Ivy with her eyes wide open. Poppy gazed over at me, twirling her hair super fast.

The weight was now in my chest. With my heart pounding, I watched as Mr Timberlac ran, pretending to chase someone. I felt like *I* was being chased. My hands and body were all sweaty.

I quickly answered all the questions as best as I could, then sneaked out my C Ho Co La Te notebook, opening it to a blank page. With the tiniest handwriting, I scribbled the answers. When I tore out the piece of paper, it made a sound. *Rrrippp.*

Mr Timberlac stopped, gyrated and looked over. I crumpled the paper in my fist as he walked toward me. The knot in my chest tightened, and I had a hard time breathing.

Ivy put up her hand. "Mr T., I have a question." As she spoke to him, I handed Poppy my answers.

She grasped the note and started scribbling. After several minutes she dropped the piece of paper on the floor and slid it to Ivy with her foot. I caught a glimpse of Olive looking my way with a confused look on her face. The mass in my chest dropped to my gut.

The next thing I knew, the test was over. I looked for the cheat sheet, which had fallen below Suzy's desk. I hastily stuffed it into my bag. Poppy turned to wink at me, and I ignored the concrete in my stomach.

After school we went to Poppy's. As soon as the door opened, a sweet and citrusy scent filled my nose. Poppy's mom was in the kitchen, whipping up something in a bowl. "Hi, girls." She pointed toward a package on the table. "It's from Dad."

Poppy sprang for it and opened it to find a book. The silhouette of a girl graced the cover. "Where is he?"

"Dad had to leave for his next trip."

Her back slouched. "He told me he'd wait for me." Ivy and Suzy stared at her with puzzled expressions. Poppy briskly pulled out her phone. "Let's dress up and have a photo shoot!" She held up her phone and mimicked a photographer while Ivy and Suzy assumed vogue-like poses. Within seconds they were out of sight.

I was about to follow them when Poppy's mom called me over. "Thank you for helping Poppy study. You're a really good friend." The mass in my stomach twisted, and I stared down at the pitcher of freshly squeezed orange juice in front of me.

Before I could ask for some, she was pouring me a cup.

"What are you making?" I asked.

"Cranberry-orange muffins, for a fundraiser." She held up a large tray. "I'm making more. Why don't you head up to Poppy's room, and I'll call you when they're done."

I wanted to stay. "Could I watch you make them?"

"Sure." She picked up a bowl. "I've put two cups of flour, two teaspoons of baking powder and a pinch of salt in here." She picked up another bowl. "And in here I've whipped together two eggs, a cup of sugar and a half cup of melted butter." She held up a half-cut orange and a hand juicer. "Do you mind?"

"Not at all!" I squeezed, accidentally squirting myself in the face. I giggled and Poppy's mom smiled. Then she measured a cup of the orange juice and poured it into the egg mixture.

"Now for the secret to making moist muffins with the right amount of fluff." She winked. "Dig a trough in the dry ingredients before adding the wet ingredients. That way you don't end up over-stirring." She poured the orange mixture into the flour and blended the whole thing together. Once everything was mixed, she stirred in the cranberries.

I helped her pour the batter into the muffin pans. She placed the trays into the oven and dusted her hands. "Now we wait. I'll call you when they're ready."

I still didn't want to leave. "Is it okay if I copy down the recipe?"

She handed me her recipe book with the page open. I pulled out my C Ho Co La Te notebook and a pen.

As the muffins baked, I took my time writing down every word as neatly as possible. She sat down across from me, placing two cups of tea on the counter. "Is this your first time baking?"

I shook my head. "My mom and I bake shortbread cookies every Christmas Eve. She dunks them in melted chocolate for me and my dad . . ." I trailed off, feeling my face tighten.

Poppy's mom lowered her cup, her expression tinged with concern. "Is everything alright?"

I looked into her kind eyes and inhaled the smell of the muffins. "Everything is perfect," I said, folding the recipe and putting it in my bag.

Poppy came down and peered into the oven. "When will they be ready?" She looked at me, surprised. "Oh you're still down here?" I didn't know if I should be relieved or upset that she hadn't noticed. Poppy headed back upstairs and I stayed.

The oven timer rang shortly after. Poppy's mom placed four muffins on a plate and handed it to me. "Thanks," I said and headed upstairs. I felt warm inside like the bottom of the plate. As soon as I stepped through the bedroom doorway, Poppy's head whipped around in my direction.

"We just got an invitation to *the* Halloween party!" she exclaimed.

"Everyone's gonna be there," Suzy said excitedly.

Ivy glared at Suzy. "Well everyone who's *cool*."

"Where's the party?" I asked.

Poppy showed me the invitation on her phone. "It's at Britannia Shipyards. Thelma Major, an eleventh grader, is throwing the party. She's known to throw the most extravagant parties. There's no way my mom's gonna let me go without adult supervision. Could I say I'm with you, Books?"

"You want me to come to the party with you?"

"I just want my mom to think that I'm at your place. She really likes you and trusts you. She says you're smart and that you're a good influence. If she knows I'm with you, she won't ask any questions."

"Um . . ." The last thing I wanted to do was lie to Poppy's mom. "I don't think . . ."

She scrolled to a page with the invitee list. Sam Garrison, Heidi Hung, Scott Ikeda and, right where she pointed, Cole James. "Come on, Books. This could be my last chance. The winner of the meet and greet is chosen on Halloween. You know I wouldn't ask if it wasn't so important."

The weight ground into my shoulders.

"What if one of your parents calls?" I asked.

Ivy huffed. "Nobody's gonna call you."

Poppy placed a hand on my shoulder. "Except us, of course. We'll let you know how the party is."

I think she knew I couldn't say no to her.

As I walked home, I pondered. What would have happened if I'd said no? Would they still hang out with me? Would they still like me? *Have they ever liked me?*

NEWTON'S THIRD LAW

For every interaction between two objects, there is a pair of equal forces acting on each other in opposite directions.

The day before Halloween, the phone rang and Poppy's number lit up on call display. *She changed her mind about inviting me.*

"Hey, Books. About the party . . ."

"Yes." My heart raced with excitement.

"I had this fairy costume ready to go, but I snagged the tights. Then it dawned on me. I should wear something that makes me stand out in front of Cole. There'll be so many fairies. What do you think I should dress as?"

My first thought was just wear what's comfortable. Then I made an excuse for having to go. "Hey, Poppy, I have something on the stove. Will call you right back."

I hung up the phone and called George. "If Poppy could dress as anything to stand out in front of Cole, what would you suggest?"

"Hmm. You know that commercial he was in?"

"*Stretcheeeeesy?*"

"It was a memorable experience for him."

"You want her to dress as cheese?" I doubted she would

go for that, but then I started thinking about some of the things Cole had told me about himself: his favourite food was pizza, which has lots of cheese. His favourite colour was sunset orange, the same colour as *Stretcheeeeesy*. Maybe it could work. With all the memories of Mom I'd been having, I understood the power of nostalgia. "Okay thanks." I was about to hang up . . .

"Wait," George said. "You told me earlier that Poppy likes books. What's her favourite book?"

"Are You There God? It's Me, Margaret. She mentioned she likes the revamped cover with a text message to God. Why do you want to know?"

"To make sure Cole and Poppy are on the same page."

Poppy's going to ask for the next page of my book. "What can Poppy do at the party to get Cole to ask her out?"

A pause.

"Well are you gonna hit me with something science-y?" asked George.

I walked around looking for ideas and rammed into a chair. "Ow!" I dropped the phone but could hear George's muffled voice on the other end. "Are you okay?"

It got me thinking. I bumped the chair and the chair bumped me back. "Newton's third law!" I picked up the phone. "Every action has a reaction with equal force, in the opposite direction."

Another pause.

"Tell Poppy to shove Cole and see if he shoves her back."

I felt my face scrunch up. "I'm no expert, but I don't think pushing someone is going to help."

"It's a classic flirting technique, don't you know?"

"I mean, I guess I've heard of a friendly elbow or something."

I hung up and called Poppy back. "You know that cheese commercial that Cole was in?"

"Yes of course! He got so many followers after that."

"He has really good memories of that time. I know it's a *stretch* from your usual wardrobe, but why don't you dress as *Stretcheeeeesy*?" I clenched my jaw.

"What?"

I could tell by the tone of her voice that she wasn't too excited about the idea.

"You'll be sure to stand out!"

"I don't know . . ."

"Senses are connected to the limbic system of the brain, where emotions are housed."

"Huh?"

"Nostalgia. You know how sometimes you smell a scent, hear a song or see something that brings back a good memory?" I remembered what Poppy told me earlier. "Kind of like when you're surrounded by books, you feel closer to your dad."

"Hmm . . . I guess. I do have some orange material."

"The Halloween party will be the perfect time to kick things up a notch with Cole."

"I'm listening," said Poppy.

"Newton's third law states that every action has a reaction in the opposite direction. Give Cole a friendly push and see if he pushes you back."

Poppy seemed to understand immediately. "Oh like flirt with him? Finally!"

"Yes, exactly." I guess George did know what he was talking about.

After we hung up, I felt restless and scanned my bookshelf for something to read. I reached for an old science textbook from Dad, and a photo of Olive and me dressed as crayons fell out. Halloween was a big deal for us. Three years ago we went as hot chocolate and a marshmallow—me as the hot chocolate and Olive as the marshmallow. Two years ago we dressed up as emojis—she was "silly" and I was "happy." Last year she went as black licorice and I went as red.

I missed her.

Surely she couldn't still be mad at me. I picked up the phone . . . then put it back and headed to the computer.

"Olive, how are you?" I typed.

Delivered. I inhaled deeply.

Seen. My heart raced.

. . .

She's writing me back.

The dots disappeared as quickly as they appeared.

"Do you want to go trick-or-treating?"

. . .

The dots appeared for longer but then stopped.

"This could be our last year. We're getting older."

A long pause.

She's thinking about it.

. . .

This time she took longer to type.

I was hopeful.

I waited.

And waited.

The dots vanished.

"Look, I'm sorry if you're still upset."

. . .

"Hear me out, it really wasn't a big deal."

. . .

. . .

. . .

"I heard the meet and greet is going to be live at the VTVZ studio!"

I waited.

Olive went offline.

"If you decide to go trick-or-treating, you know where to find me."

ATMOSPHERIC PRESSURE

The pressure exerted by the weight of the atmosphere.

Halloween landed on a Saturday, which was also the day of the party. Olive never returned my messages about trick-or-treating. I turned on the television and flicked through the channels: a bunch of Halloween specials, a fishing show and a commercial about peer pressure that preached things like "You have a choice." My body squirmed, so I turned off the television.

A bowl of mini chocolate bars sat at our front entrance along with several empty wrappers. I ate a few and let the sweetness linger on my tongue . . . until a putrid smell entered my nostrils.

I pinched my nose and dashed into the kitchen. "Yuck, what is that?"

Dad's eyes shifted to the desiccator. "I'm making natto."

Fermented soybeans with the smell of rotten garbage and the consistency of slimy snot. "Why?"

"For one, it's healthy. It's good for your bones, your heart and your immune system. And I needed something gooey.

I'm making guts and brains for dinner." His hips swayed and his feet swivelled like the old days.

"Have you talked to Mom?"

He paused.

"Is she getting my messages?"

"She's . . . sorry she's been so busy." He turned away. "But she sent you something." He left the room and came back with a box set of Make Your Own Slime.

It seemed more like something Dad would get me, not Mom. But then he added, "She sends her love."

A wave of relief washed over me. *I guess I was always out when she called.* "Did she mention when she's coming home?"

"She said she'll talk to you soon." His head turned toward the counter. Seeing him with his collection of beakers, test tubes and micro spatulas, I couldn't help feeling a tinge of warmth.

"Can I help?" I asked.

"Aren't you going trick-or-treating? With Olive?"

"Not this year."

"Really? I didn't think you'd give up a chance to bring home a bag full of candy and *chocolates*."

"Are you sure you're not just tricking me to get you the chocolates?" I gave him a knowing grin.

"I just know how much you love this time of year."

I did. *I do.* "Maybe I will go."

I went back to my room to search for a costume. Going through my closet and drawers in the eleventh hour was like finding the perfect outfit for the first day of school.

I pulled out the lab coat and goggles Mom sent me, and put them on, but it wasn't a disguise—I still looked like me. *Ouch.* I stepped on a tile from Elementabble, a hydrogen H.

I had an idea. I wrote a large letter O onto a red shirt. Then I cut two large circles out of a white shirt, wrapped them around two cantaloupe-sized balloons and wrote the letter H on each one before attaching them to the shoulders of the red shirt. "There," I said, holding up my homemade costume, H_2O—water. Then I added some H_2O along with some of my homemade fertilizer to my experimental plants. They were fighting to stay alive.

With the remaining fabric, I made myself a mask and looked in the mirror. My inflated shoulders and mask made

me look a bit like a superhero, but it was pretty decent for a last-minute costume.

Dad saw me on the way out and gave me a thumbs up. "Enjoy your guts and brains for dinner," I hollered, and left.

The houses were decorated with carved pumpkins, ghosts, witches and ghouls. The air smelled of decomposing leaves and burning pumpkins, accompanied by the occasional booms and crackling sounds of fireworks.

All the ingredients for a really fun Halloween. But something was missing. Trick-or-treating just wasn't the same without Olive. I walked past her house, wondering if she was home or if she too went out. We always planned our route around the string of townhouses near her place— more value for distance travelled. Maybe I'd run into her there. If I could just catch her in a good mood and explain exactly what happened, *I'm sure she'd understand.*

I followed a robot, ladybug and cat around the townhouses. When I came back out onto the street, I saw a house on the corner that had a huge pot on the balcony with smoke coming out of it: witch's brew, made of dry ice and water. Loud noises blared from the door as a group of people went in.

Poppy said she'd call me from the party. *I'd better head home.*

By the time I walked through my front door, I'd polished off over a dozen pieces of chocolate from my bag and my head ached. I guzzled down a glass of water and was re-filling it when Poppy's number lit up on call display. *Just in time.* "Hello," I said and took a sip.

"Hi, Emma."

I spat out the water. "H-Hi, Mrs Sinclair." I covered the speaker on the phone so she wouldn't hear my pounding heart.

"Could I talk to Poppy? She forgot her cellphone at home."

My mind whizzed around like a deflating balloon. "Pardon me?"

"Could you put Poppy on the phone?"

"Umm . . . you know what, she went to pick up something from the corner store."

"This late? What did she need? Did she go alone?" She shot off questions like pop rocks.

"Ah . . . she was craving popcorn and we didn't have any." I clamped my lips together to mute my lies. "I'm sure she's fine." The words just slipped out. My hand draped over my mouth.

"Could you have her call me when she gets back? And take down my number, just in case you need to call me." With a shaky hand, I jotted it down on a piece of paper.

We hung up, and I felt sick to my stomach. Poppy's mom wasn't just anyone. She made me feel more at home than anyone else. I stared at the number on the piece of paper. Before I knew it, I had folded it into a tiny origami fish.

How was I going to reach Poppy? She didn't have her cell, and I didn't have Ivy's or Suzy's number. I circled the room wondering what I could do. What if something happened? I unravelled the origami fish and thought about calling back Poppy's mom. Then I refolded it—I didn't want to be a tattletale.

I grabbed an issue of *Science Today and Tomorrow* and read about atmospheric pressure. A graph showed images of famous mountains, ranging from Ben Nevis to Mount Everest; as the mountains got higher, their atmospheric pressures lowered.

It wasn't making me feel any better. I sat down and hugged my knees, rocking back and forth as the air around me squeezed my body. The pressure was building, becoming too much. *Atmospheric pressure decreases with elevation.*

I sprinted out the door searching for the tallest thing I could find. I kept running, but nothing was remotely high enough. Steveston was as flat as the prairies.

Finally I settled for a staircase near the empty developments and climbed it as fast as I could. When I got to the top I just stood there, listening to the music booming from the shipyards, where the party was.

I lied to Poppy's mom. I told her that Poppy was fine, but what if she was actually in trouble? I couldn't just sit around doing nothing. I put my mask back on and headed toward the music.

NEWTON'S THIRD LAW IN ACTION

The laws of physics don't always apply.

As I neared Britannia Shipyards, fireworks flashed and lit up the sky. The air was cool, but my body was on fire from all the running.

When I got to the party, a live band was on stage. The ruckus of the music and the shouting and laughter mingled with the smell of damp wood, popcorn and warm bodies. Everyone wore a costume—many dressed as characters from the *Magical Creatures* series: fairies, goblins and wizards. I saw a fancy popcorn machine, a cotton candy maker and even a photo booth in the corner. Poppy wasn't kidding—this was an extravagant party.

A bunch of pixies came out of the photo booth, and I heard Ivy's voice coming from the one holding a wand. "You blocked my face with your wings!"

"Sorry," said the pixie who I knew was Suzy.

From the corner of my eye, I spotted something orange. Poppy twirled her hair, which poked out from her cheese costume. She took photos of the pixies from the side but didn't seem too eager to join them. If anything, it looked like she was avoiding them. Did she regret dressing as cheese? My throat felt dry as salt.

I was about to walk up to her but remembered: *she doesn't know I'm here.* Poppy was safe. At least I didn't lie to her mom about that. I decided to go home before she recognized me.

On my way out I saw a table with two punch bowls. I was so thirsty I couldn't resist. One had eyeballs made of lychees and blueberries, and the other had finger-like objects with a prickle of fake blood. I quickly turned away, only to see a guy stagger toward me with a knife stuck in his head. The blood trickling down his face made me queasy. *It's fake, don't faint.*

I stumbled outside and took a seat on a bench, inhaling the cold air. After reciting the first twenty-seven elements of the periodic table, I felt better.

A guy wearing a goblin costume sat down beside me, holding a bag of popcorn. He readjusted his mask, and I saw a glimpse of his face.

"Cole?"

"Is that you, Emma?" He looked up and down at my costume. "What are you?"

"A water molecule."

"Oh . . ." He snickered.

"At least my costume's original." I stuck my tongue out at him.

"Exactly why I wore this, because it's *not* original. I can sit back, relax and not be bothered by anyone." He propped his mask on top of his head and ate some popcorn. "Want some? It's cheddar and caramel."

"Such a waste of space, these cheddar ones." I pushed them out of the way and fished out the caramel-covered ones.

Cole took another handful. "The salty cheddar *makes* the popcorn," he said, shovelling it in his mouth.

I wasn't surprised. After all, he did star in a cheese commercial. "I'd pick sweet over salty any day," I said.

"So you'd eat an apple over french fries?"

"Only if the apple's smothered in chocolate or caramel."

He cracked a smile. "We used to make caramel apples for Halloween. It's always been my favourite holiday." He grabbed the mask off his head and spun it around. "When I was little, I used to love dressing up and performing. That's probably why my parents put me in acting school."

"But you don't seem to like being around a lot of people."

"True, but for some reason I'm comfortable on camera."
Then he turned toward me. "What's your favourite holiday?"

"It used to be Halloween, but I miss Christmas more."

"What do you mean?" Something about his eyes made it
easy for me to talk to him.

"It's my mom's favourite time of the year. She deco-
rates the house all festive, and we have our traditions like
baking chocolate-covered shortbread and playing board
games. I'm just looking extra forward to it this year. My
mom's been away."

"I know what you mean. My parents travel a lot with
my younger brother. He's the star of our family, so basically . . ."
He met my gaze. "I'm looking forward to some family time
too."

Other than the noise from the party, there was silence
between us.

"So what were you doing sitting out here alone?"

"The sight of blood makes me nauseous, even if it's not
real. I'm avoiding anyone with a hint of anything that looks
like blood."

"I'm avoiding someone too," he admitted. "I get nightmares about a certain commercial I . . ."

We were interrupted by a guy dressed as Wentworth
the Wizard setting off fireworks. He flicked a rod and it
snaked toward us before sprouting up in the air.

Cole quickly shielded me. His hand landed on the back
of my neck, and a tingle went through my body. I swallowed an awkward breath before pulling away. If Poppy

were to see me with Cole like this, she'd freak out. "I have to go!" I said, and took off.

I was so flustered I bumped into someone dressed as a book. The front page flapped open and a face was revealed. "George?"

"Oh hey, Emma." He looked concerned about something. "Poppy asked about you and me. I think she might be on to us."

"Don't worry." I swatted the air. "Poppy thinks we're going out."

"What? Why would she think that?"

"I had to tell her something to keep her from finding out that you're helping me."

George looked like he'd seen a ghost. He grasped his face with all ten fingers and let them slide down his face.

"What's wrong?"

"Poppy can't think we're together." He paced up and down in his book costume, which kept flapping open and shut.

I looked at the cover. It had a couple of text messages on it. "Are You There God?" I read out loud, head spinning. "Wait . . . I told you Poppy loves that book. You don't have a thing for her, do you?"

He froze.

I froze.

Things started to dawn on me: George asked a lot of questions about Poppy. He observed the interactions between Poppy and Cole almost too intently. And his advice never really made sense. Images flooded back of Cole getting hit by a shoe, George coming over to Poppy's with a book about makeup, Poppy dressed as . . .

Wait! Cole was avoiding someone or something from a commercial he'd been in. Could it be . . .? Panic kicked in. "George, you didn't tell me to tell Poppy to dress as *Stretcheeeeesy* because you knew Cole has nightmares about it?"

George bit his lips. "I told you the cheese ad was a memorable experience for him. I didn't say it was a *good* memory." He turned away like he was dodging a grenade.

"How could you!" I crossed my arms, and one of the balloons on my shoulders popped. *Oh no, Newton's third law.*

I searched frantically for Poppy inside . . . outside . . . then back inside again. There was no sign of her.

She must have gone home. She probably couldn't stand being in that cheese costume. She must have been boiling hot, not to mention that she wouldn't have recognized Cole anyway. He wore a mask—like half the people here. I convinced myself everything would be okay and started to leave.

The air was now colder, and fewer people were outside. A group of guys were setting off fireworks. One soared high through the air, screeching, and another illuminated the boardwalk. Then I saw . . .

Poppy dressed as cheese.

And Cole, with his mask propped on top of his head, face fully exposed.

It was too late. Poppy spotted Cole.

She lurched toward him. The fear on his face was like he was about to be pounced on by a bear. Poppy went to shove him . . . everything was in slow motion.

I couldn't watch.

I ran away.

FRICTION

A force that works against the direction of movement.

The weekend was over and dark clouds loomed outside, kind of like my own cloud of doom.

I forced myself to go to school. In the hallway I heard Poppy from behind me. "Books!" The anger in her voice pierced my ears, but I sprinted down the hallway, pretending not to hear her.

From the other end, George called out, "Emma!"

Ugh! How could George betray me? I was so mad at him I bolted down another hallway with my eyes stapled to the ground.

"No running!" yelled Godzilla. I stopped, then speed-walked to the stairwell and hid beneath it. I pulled out a crinkled issue of *Science Today and Tomorrow,* opened it randomly and tried to concentrate on an article. It talked about friction—a force resisting motion—and how walking or running requires it between the shoes and the floor. I read that friction acts to grip the ground, which prevents sliding and gets you to your destination. It was kind of ironic, since friction was also the very thing that slowed you down from getting there.

I heard Olive's voice. She was talking to Molly and Holly.

"They chose the winner of the meet and greet," said Molly.

"I'm so bummed," huffed Holly.

"Me too. I would have done *anything* to win," said Olive.

Phew—at least I didn't win. I couldn't imagine having to choose between Poppy and Olive right now. They were both so mad at me. *How can I make it up to them?*

At lunchtime I convinced myself to go to the cafeteria. I just needed to talk to Olive . . . to Poppy, to explain to them what happened.

Olive sat with Molly and Holly, giggling. She seemed to be in a good mood. I took a step toward her. George intervened by taking a seat with them, and I halted, pretending to look for something in my bag.

As I pulled out my C Ho Co La Te notebook, several pieces of paper flew out. I picked one up to find one of my terrible attempts at drawing the Momo Kesho logo, which George was so keen on designing. How did I miss that he was totally into Poppy? I gathered the rest of the papers and made a mental note to clean my bag.

Hair guy and breakdancer guy sat together, watching Poppy, Ivy and Suzy. Poppy turned her head toward me suddenly, and my stomach curdled like spoiled milk.

Then her face lit up with a smile. Heart leaping, I took a step toward her until I realized the smile wasn't for me.

Cole stood behind me. "Hey."

"Hi," I replied, stomach still churning.

"It was nice talking to you at the party."

I turned toward Poppy, and a flash of hurt spread across her face. *Oh no! What if she thinks I set the whole thing up to fail? She can't see me talking to Cole.* "Sorry, I ate something funny and don't feel well." Holding my stomach, I ran off and decided to avoid him from then on.

After school I walked to the dock, where Poppy and I first met. What was I thinking, pretending I knew anything about boys? How could I lie to her and think I could get away with it? I'd dug myself into a hole so deep, I couldn't crawl out of it.

Something bopped up in the water. It was Saul the sea lion. He floated on his backside like he was sunbathing. Maybe if she hadn't fallen in the water that day, we would have been fine.

Suddenly Saul's eyes opened, and he glared at me like he knew I was an imposter. I thought about coming clean to Poppy. *I don't know much about guys, so George helped me. It was clearly a mix-up.*

I imagined her saying, "I don't need you." The words ate away at me.

"Books!" Poppy's voice pulled me out of my thoughts. I jerked back, thinking she was going to push me in the water.

"I . . . I'm so . . ."

"You're never going to believe what happened at the party." Surprisingly, Poppy's voice was calm. "I was about to give Cole a friendly shove, when he yelped and ran away. I was so embarrassed, so mad . . . at you." A glimmer appeared on her face. "But then George told me."

I was confused. "Told you what?"

"That Cole was not running away from *me*. He was running away from the guy dressed as a mouse. Cole's apparently scared of mice."

"What?" My jaw dropped open.

"The guy in the mouse suit was pretending to chase the cheese: me. So when I ran up to Cole, he saw the mouse, not me."

"George told you all this?"

"Yeah. He even confirmed what you said, that Cole loves cheese."

What?

Her lips puckered. "You're so lucky to have a boyfriend who cares so much about you and your friends."

I couldn't understand. Did George feel bad? Was he actually trying to help me? Or was he up to no good again? Either way, I went along with it. "I guess I am."

"So what were you and Cole talking about in the cafeteria?"

"Um . . ." I totally lied. "He actually asked me about you."

"Really?"

Think fast. Poppy kept twirling her hair. "He thinks you have really nice hair."

She flicked her curls and smiled, but her grin slipped off her face. "I thought maybe he liked someone else."

"Why would you think that?"

"I saw him talking to another girl at the party. He had his mask off, but the girl had her back to me. She looked like some sort of superhero."

Gulp.

"They talked closely and for quite a while. When I finally worked up enough courage to go talk to him, I saw Cole clasping the back of her neck."

The fireworks.

"I didn't know if he was gonna kiss her or what, so I turned back."

I swallowed another lump. "I'm sure it's all a misunderstanding."

She gazed up with her hand on her forehead, like she was losing hope.

I can't let her give up. She won't need me anymore. "I have a plan," I blurted out even though I didn't.

"You've said that before."

I needed more time to think. "Give me till the weekend, and I won't let you down."

"Fine, but last chance, okay? Desperate is not a good look for me."

"Okay, last chance."

The weekend was fast approaching and I still needed something. *Mom would know what to do.* Why hadn't she returned my calls? Maybe her phone was broken. I decided to email her.

"Dear Mom,

Could you please call me back. It's urgent!"

I deleted it and tried again.

"Mom, I want to ask you something."

I hated writing emails for something so important.

"I would love your advice. I have a friend who is interested in this boy. What do you suggest she do?"

Call me. Xoxo Emma."

There . . . send.

I nervously scrolled up and down my messages, hoping she would write back right away. I tried to keep myself busy with a bunch of science articles, but I couldn't stop checking my inbox. Then I went through my junk mail, scanning the subject lines. *"Congratulations, Emma Sakamoto!"*

My first thought was that it was a scam. But then I recognized the sender's logo and clicked open the message.

"You won the contest to meet the cast of the Magical Creatures *TV show."*

I'm the winner? I reread the message. *". . . Up close and personal with the cast . . . watch Wentworth the Wizard perform magic . . . Empress Octavia and her signature move . . . exclusive seat on stage . . ."*

Oh no, I'm definitely the winner. My mind swirled like a whirlpool as I thought of Poppy and Olive. After what happened at the Halloween party, Poppy could definitely use the winning ticket. Being on stage with Cole would finally allow her to get the attention she wanted. But then again, giving it to Olive would mean so much to her. It could smooth things over between us. Olive was a bigger fan of the show, but Poppy was a bigger fan of Cole. Olive wanted it more, but Poppy needed it more. Or maybe it was the other way around. How was I supposed to choose?

Nobody's seen this message. I'll just keep it a secret.

EXOTHERMIC REACTION

A chemical process that releases energy as heat or light.

On Saturday I went to meet Poppy at Maritime Anytime. Still having no idea what advice to give her, I anxiously pushed the ship's steering wheel on the door to open it. She was already there with her head buried in a book. On the cover was an image of a bunch of scrabble tiles.

She looked up to wave, with excitement on her face. What was I thinking—coming here with no plan? I had one last chance. *She's going to expect something ground-breaking.*

She dove back into her book. "Just finishing up this part; it's getting so good."

I couldn't stop sweating, so I quickly picked up an issue of *Science Today and Tomorrow* and flipped through it while searching for inspiration. I stopped at a page with a list of reactions that give off heat, like detergent in water, baking soda in vinegar and rusting iron.

Poppy put down her book and the lump in my throat returned. I convinced her that we needed hot chocolates, and we walked to the café side. She got hers topped with a swirl of whipped cream and a piece of chocolate in the shape of a nautical star. I got a lactose-free version, which didn't come with either.

We sat on a bench with an anchor painted on it, and I could tell she was waiting for me to say something.

I pointed to her drink. "That looks nice."

Poppy gaped, as if she had an idea, and pulled out her phone. She took a photo of her hot cocoa with bookshelves in the background and tapped her screen as she uttered, "Maritime Anytime, a hidden gem in Steveston Village."

I wondered why she would post a place that was a hidden gem. Wouldn't she prefer it to stay that way? *I know I do.*

"I read online that . . ." Poppy began when her phone dinged.

Oh no, what if they announced the winner online and she knows? My stomach twisted and turned like it was in a washing machine.

She put down her phone. "I read that Cole likes smart girls."

Phew, she doesn't know.

"I thought if I posted a photo of this place, full of books, he would like my photo." Then she looked right at me as if I had the answer to her problem.

"Cole thinks you have pretty hair," I reminded her.

"Why hasn't he told *me* that?"

"He can be a little shy."

"But he's an actor."

"That doesn't mean he's not a private person." Her expression told me she needed something more. "What do you think has worked best so far?"

"There was the shoe in the air."

I gulped.

"The red gown and gold heels."

I bit my lip.

"That time we played the video game together when Cole and George came over."

Oh George. Now I feel like I owe her the ticket. Just keep asking questions.

"What do you like most about Cole?"

"For one, he's gorgeous. Don't you think?"

He did have gorgeous eyes—ones that pull you in. I clasped my head. *Keep it together, Emma.* "What else?"

Her phone dinged, and she immediately pulled it out. "He hasn't liked it yet. Nobody's liked it." She sighed.

"Liked what?"

"The photo I just posted."

"You *just* posted it."

"Oh no, I lost a follower." She pushed her phone toward me like she was asking me to take it away. "It's way too stressful. If you don't post, you're irrelevant. If you do, you wait for others to approve. The whole thing's messed up." Then she said the strangest thing. "Books, I'm jealous of you."

Why would Poppy be jealous of me?

"You don't have a phone. I'd feel so free without one."

"Why don't you just take a break from it?"

"I can't. I have FOMO."

"Huh?"

"Fear of missing out." She took back her phone and started swiping again. "I have this need to keep up to date with everything and everyone. If I don't see what's going on, I feel out of it. But if I see that I've missed something, I feel left out. You can't win."

It made sense. Since I'd met Poppy, I didn't want to miss out on things either. She was confiding in me, and I finally felt I could confide in her. "Remember how I told you about my mom?"

"Thank goodness for moms!" She shuffled through her bag. "I couldn't imagine going through, you know, all these changes without her. Ah, there it is." She pulled out a maxi pad.

Just thinking about needing one of those made me dizzy.

A hint of pity entered her voice. "I forgot your mom's away. Well you always have me if you have any questions about stuff."

I instantly lit up. She gave me this heartfelt smile as she walked to the restroom, and I really felt like we were forming a true friendship. Maybe I should tell Poppy I won the ticket— offer to give it to her. She wouldn't have to worry about Cole so much.

When Poppy returned I took a sip of my cocoa, ready to tell her. I put down the cup and the double helix on my DNA bracelet pinged the table. It reminded me of how close Olive and I used to be. A pang of guilt hit me. If I gave the ticket to Poppy, Olive would be devastated. Then

I imagined giving it to Olive, and the thought of her excited face made my whole body warm. I had to find some other way to get Poppy and Cole together.

"Why don't you become friends with Cole first," I suggested, "and let the rest come naturally."

"Hmm. But how? I get so nervous around him." She stared helplessly out the window. Then her gaze shifted, and I turned my head to see Ivy and Suzy saunter in.

"Hi, Poppy," said Ivy without acknowledging me. Just as I wondered how they found out about this place, Suzy said they'd seen Poppy's post.

Ivy gripped my shoulder firmly, and I thought she was going to dig her nails into me. "Would you mind getting me a hot chocolate, extra whip? I'll pay you back." Her voice was nice enough, but then she squeezed between Poppy and me, and I fell off my seat.

"Same for me," said Suzy.

By the time I got back, they had decided to go to the mall. Ivy pointed her head toward the door. "Let's go." Suzy got up right away, but Poppy was on her phone again. When she put it away, they went out the door. I remained standing with a cup of cocoa in each hand. I put them down and followed.

On the way to the bus stop, someone with a puffy jacket, hood fastened tightly around their face, walked toward us. The others passed right by, but as I got near I knew who it was. I wanted to say something to Olive, and stopped.

"We're gonna miss the bus," Ivy shouted and kept walking away.

Suzy rubbed her hands together as she followed. "It's freezing." Poppy kept walking with her eyes glued to her phone.

I waved my hand. "Go ahead without me." They did, without hesitation.

Olive and I looked at each other for a while. There was a sadness in her eyes, and I knew she wanted to make up. I was about to tell her how much I missed her when she pulled out a crinkled note. From the chocolate bar squares to the tiny scribbles, I knew exactly what it was. "Where did you get that?"

"I found it on the ground. I knew something was going on the day of the test, but I never thought you would . . ."

I went to grab the note but she pulled away. "You could get into big trouble for this."

Anger sparked. "Only if you say something!"

"Look, I'm just trying to help you."

"If you were, you'd give it back and not say a word." I held out my hand.

"I know you, Emma. This isn't you."

"How would you even know? You've clearly been avoiding me."

"Why would you want to hang out with people who'd make you do this kind of stuff?"

"Nobody made me do anything." Heat climbed up my spine. "Why won't you just give it back?"

"What's wrong with you?"

"What's wrong with *you*?" My face burned and the words erupted out of my mouth. "You're jealous. You can't

stand the fact that I'm friends with girls who are more popular than you!"

The colour drained from Olive's face, and I couldn't look her in the eyes.

I never thought Olive would make me feel like that. *To think I was going to give her the winning ticket.*

CELLULAR RESPIRATION

A biochemical pathway that utilizes food and oxygen to provide energy to the cells.

I managed to catch the bus with Poppy, Ivy and Suzy. As soon as we entered the mall, it began to feel a lot like Christmas. A large tree stood tall in the centre of the main entrance, ready to be decorated. Ribbons and bells were being hung from the vaulted ceilings. Poppy pulled out her phone and uttered, "Checking in at Richmond Centre. The seasons are changing and so is my wardrobe." She turned to me and smiled.

I smiled back. *I don't need Olive. I have other friends now.*

We walked through a few stores before entering Poppy's favourite. Right away, Suzy grabbed a coral-coloured sweater. "Try this on, Poppy. It'll look great on you."

Ivy shoved a purple sweater in between them. "Try this instead. It's more your colour."

Poppy didn't take either and skimmed through the racks. I saw a flash of vibrant colours: red, green, white and silver, coming from a table stacked with festive sweaters. I had a sudden flashback of Mom bringing home matching

Christmas sweaters for me and Dad. She said they were dorky, like us, but in an endearing way. When she took off her jacket, we saw that she was wearing the same one. Mom firmly believed that Christmas was a time to cherish with family.

I yanked out a sweater that unfolded to show a giant gingerbread cookie dancing with a reindeer. Real bells adorned the sleeves from shoulder to wrist. To my surprise, Poppy took it from my hand, pulled it over her head and chuckled as the bells jingled. I put on a sweater with Santa's head popping out of a wreath. Poppy and I made funny faces in the mirror and laughed at ourselves.

Ivy's eyes rolled so high I thought they'd disappear. "I'm getting hungry," she said. "Let's go to the food court."

Poppy, Ivy and Suzy went straight for the pizza, but I craved something sweet. I headed to the crêpe station to get a non-dairy one with a chocolate spread.

As I waited in line, I looked over at the others. Their heads were so close together, it was as if they were eating the same slice of pizza.

I got to the front of the line only to realize that I didn't have enough money.

When I got back to the table, their heads immediately splayed apart. "What are you talking about?" I asked.

"We're gonna get some nail polish," Ivy said.

Oh is that all?

When we got to the pharmacy, Poppy, Ivy and Suzy headed straight for the cosmetics section. They pulled out a few colours, painting their fingernails with the testers.

They held out their hands, admiring them.

Poppy grasped a bottle of turquoise in one hand and gold in the other. Ivy held two shades of purple in one hand and a large bottle of cover-up in the other. Suzy grabbed a red lipstick to match the nail polish she had.

"Red doesn't suit you," scoffed Ivy, and Suzy immediately exchanged the reds for grey nail polish and a tinted lip gloss.

Poppy handed me a bottle of nail polish labelled "Princess Pink." I took it even though I knew I didn't have enough money.

When I looked up, Ivy and Suzy were walking toward the till. "Are you coming?" Poppy asked.

"Um . . ." I paused and gripped the bottle. "I don't actually have . . ."

Before I could finish, Poppy slid back and whispered, "Take it." All their hands were empty. That's when I realized they were *not* walking toward the till.

My breath quickened. I felt like my oxygen supply was cut off, and I had no energy to think. Hands trembling, I stuffed the little bottle in the deepest corner of my pocket and followed the others. A cashier rang up some toothpaste for a customer. My heart hammered so loud I was sure they could hear it.

One step. Two. I didn't dare breathe until I was safely out.

INERTIA

The tendency of an object to continue in its existing state until an external force acts upon it.

The air was unusually calm. The leaves were so still that the trees looked like they were painted. But my heart still trembled. I walked to school unable to focus on anything except the pink bottle hiding inside my pocket.

I got to English early and started reading an article about inertia: a cup stays put even though the tablecloth from underneath gets pulled away; a ball continues to roll until it's caught. *Science Today and Tomorrow* wasn't putting me at ease like it usually did.

Before I knew it, class was full. Poppy, Suzy and Ivy all had painted fingernails. Molly and Holly talked about how Cole was away on set. I looked around for Olive, but she wasn't in class.

Godzilla clapped her hands loudly to signal the start of class. Everyone stopped talking immediately. "We'll be working on some freestyle writing. Choose a topic and unleash your creative self." Chatter began but Godzilla hushed everyone again. "This is an individual assignment." Her shushing finger remained on her mouth.

Molly and Holly wrote quickly. Coding guy massaged his temples. Ivy looked at her fingernails while Suzy scratched her head. George admired Poppy, along with breakdancer guy and hair guy. Olive still wasn't there.

I was about to write a summary of the article I'd just read, but I had a hard time focusing.

"Emma!"

"Yes, Mom."

Laughter echoed throughout the classroom, and my face heated up like a thermoplate. "I mean, um, I . . ."

"Emma," Godzilla repeated, staring down at my blank paper. "See me after class."

What did she want from me? Did she find out we stole? What if she was there—did she see me put the nail polish in my pocket? With a quivering hand, I touched my pencil to the paper and tried to write something. Maybe if I admitted what I did and explained why, right here on this very page, Godzilla would understand. Every time I started writing something, I scribbled it out.

The next thing I knew, class was over, and all I had was a page of incomplete sentences and a bunch of crossed-out words.

In a surprisingly kind voice, Godzilla asked me if everything was okay. "I noticed you've been out of sorts lately. Since your last presentation, your assignments haven't been, let's say, up to par." Her eyes warmed. "You have so much potential."

For the first time ever, I felt I could talk to her. "Have you ever done anything you regretted?"

"Oh, Emma, I've done a lot of things I regret."

My breath calmed. "Like what?"

"Just this morning, I used the last coffee pod and drank the whole cup by myself. Normally my boyfriend wouldn't mind—he usually has a lot of energy—but today something was bothering him. He needed it more and I still took it."

This was hardly a problem as big as mine. But she did seem to feel bad. "What did you do about it?"

"I apologized and bought him a coffee on the way to work."

Apologizing wasn't going to help me. "What I did was *way* worse." I clasped my mouth as soon as I realized what I'd said.

"Do you want to talk about it?"

There was no way I could tell her everything I'd done. She would report me. I could see my future going down the drain. *Change topics.*

"How did you and your boyfriend meet?"

Her pointy nose wiggled. "Why do you ask?"

"I really want to help this friend who likes a guy. I want him to ask her out. But I don't know how to make it happen. I don't know much about boys."

Godzilla pulled up a seat beside me. "Why do you have to know anything about boys to help your friend?"

Huh?

"You're the one who gave a talk on the misrepresentation of girls. What about the misrepresentation of boys?"

"What do you mean?"

"Does it really matter who asks out who?"

She had a point. All this time I thought Poppy needed to get Cole's attention just so *he'd* ask *her* out. Maybe it didn't have to be that way.

"It doesn't matter who you are. All anyone really wants is to find a real connection," she said.

A real connection. "I never thought of it that way. Thanks, Ms Grimaldi."

Science class was full by the time I got there. I went straight up to Poppy, eager to tell her what I'd just learned. Mr Timberlac cut in front of me and asked me to have a seat in front of his desk. He tightened his black bow tie, with an expression much more serious than usual.

I decided to write Poppy a note. *"I have something to tell you. It's about making a real connection with Cole. Meet me after class. Emma."*

I folded the piece of paper into a square and wrote "Poppy" on the front. As I turned to pass the note, it got snatched from my fingertips. Mr Timberlac hovered over me like a willow tree. "Emma, I'd like to talk to you after class." Then he walked to the back and pointed to Poppy, Ivy and Suzy. "And to the three of you as well."

He knew.

Did Olive . . . no she wouldn't have.

But then again, why wouldn't she after what I'd said to her? I felt queasy, like I'd seen blood.

The bell rang, and the four of us waited in our seats. Mr Timberlac took a long sip of his coffee before walking up to us. "You all did very well on your test. But your open-ended answers were uncannily similar."

It wasn't Olive. I hadn't even thought about making any mistakes or changing some of our answers so they'd be different.

He crossed his arms. "Does anyone have anything to tell me?" When his eyes landed on mine, a curious look spread across his face.

None of us said a word. Poppy, Ivy and Suzy sat motionless as if they were flash frozen.

"I would like each of you to think *very* carefully about this. I'll give you a few minutes." He took his coffee and left.

"What are we gonna do?" Poppy's voice was laced with panic.

Suzy gnawed on her hand like it was corn on the cob. "My parents are gonna kill me."

"Stop being a baby, Suze!" Ivy jeered, and Suzy clamped her teeth on her knuckles.

"Maybe we should come clean," I said.

"No way!" Suzy stammered. "My parents will disown me."

"It'll be worse if Mr Timberlac finds out himself," I said.

"If he had any proof, we'd have been caught already." Not a hint of concern in Ivy's voice.

I wasn't about to tell them about the cheat sheet Olive found.

Poppy stared out the window, shaking her head from side to side, and I knew I wasn't convincing anyone.

Mr Timberlac came back in and I watched, cringing, as Ivy explained to him that it must have been a coincidence. "We studied together," she said. "And great minds think alike."

I avoided any face-to-face contact with Mr Timberlac.

That night I had a hard time falling asleep. My mind wouldn't stop racing. *What if we get caught? What if this goes on our permanent records?* I imagined myself sitting with someone from university admissions. "Emma, your grades are impeccable, but I'm afraid our school looks poorly on applicants with cheating on their record."

My whole life, I've wanted to be a scientist who made a difference in the world. When did my social life become more important? The more I thought about what had happened, the more my body tightened. I flipped from side to side, tensing and releasing different muscle groups to help me relax, a technique I'd read about called progressive muscle relaxation. I made a plank with my body until my arms gave out.

Finally I laid on my back, closed my eyes and counted sheep. But the sheep turned into a ball of wool, and the ball of wool turned into a peach. The Momo Kesho logo flashed in my head—a cosmetics brand I made up, just so they would like me.

I went to Dad's office to find something to read, hopscotching from one open spot on the floor to another until I reached his desk. I opened a drawer to find a bunch of molecules, all tangled up along with empty chocolate wrappers. In the drawer below, some more papers and a few stragglers from Elementabble. The tiles for carbon, oxygen and nitrogen, C O N, lay next to each other. I quickly jumbled the tiles with my hands and went to Dad and Mom's room.

I didn't know exactly why I went there, but it certainly wasn't for Dad's bulldozer snores. I went to Mom's closet, brushing my hands against her clothes until I felt a silky scarf. Wrapping it around my neck made me feel a little better. I took it to my room and let her scent sweep over me.

All of a sudden I heard knocking. Then pounding. My bedroom door flew open, and two cops in SWAT gear barged in. Two more climbed up my window, and I had nowhere to go. They turned my whole room upside down, emptying the drawers, ransacking the closet and throwing off my mattress, with me still lying on it. I caught my pillow, stuck my arm in the case and frantically searched for *it*. I clutched my palm tightly until they asked me to open my hand.

The Princess Pink nail polish.

I woke up in a sweaty mess.

REVERSIBLE AND IRREVERSIBLE PROCESSES

A reversible process is one in which changes can be undone. An irreversible process cannot be undone.

The next morning I felt a mix of bad emotions, like a bag of leftover jelly beans that nobody wanted, with flavours of worry, guilt and fear. I squeezed the Princess Pink nail polish tightly, as if it were to blame.

I started thinking about the cheat sheet that Olive had. How did she get it? I could have sworn I picked it up the day of the test and stuffed it into my bag. Then I remembered . . . a bunch of papers fell out of my bag at the cafeteria when I was avoiding George. *Why didn't I get rid of the evidence right away?* I had to do something to keep myself from going crazy. I dumped my backpack upside down to clean it. Most of the loose papers went straight to recycling, but there was one piece of crumpled paper with neater handwriting. It was the cranberry-orange muffin recipe that I'd copied from Poppy's mom.

This was exactly what I needed. With the side of my hand, I ironed out the recipe. I headed to the kitchen and collected ingredients: sugar, butter, eggs . . . oranges, which we didn't have.

But we did have—I opened the freezer to check . . . *yup*—a can of orange concentrate, which poked out from behind Mom's high heels. I was surprised she hadn't asked about her favourite pair of heels. *I really need to clean them before she gets back.* I tugged on them, but they were cemented to the bottom of the freezer with ice and goo. I grabbed the can of orange concentrate and placed it in a bowl of warm water. Then I measured out the dry ingredients: two cups of flour, two teaspoons of baking powder and a pinch of salt.

I shook the can of orange juice, but it still felt half-frozen. Staring at it wasn't making it thaw any faster, so I moved on to find the next ingredient: fresh cranberries. Again we didn't have fresh ones, but I saw a jar of dried cranberries on the counter. Hidden behind it was a can of orange concentrate that was completely thawed. *Dad must have forgotten about it.*

When I went to place the half-frozen can back in the freezer, the light inside flicked on, and an idea came to me. The can of partially thawed orange juice could easily be frozen again. *The process is reversible.*

That's it! I could return it. I ran to my room, grabbed the princess nail polish and dashed out the door.

The bus was stuffed like the molecular models in Dad's desk, and I was sweating profusely. As soon as we stopped at the mall, I jetted out. I had to keep going before I changed my mind. Letting my legs take charge, I made it to the pharmacy.

The second I stepped into the store, my heart thumped so loudly I could feel it in my eyeballs. I tried to move fast, but every step was like trekking through a muddy river against the flow.

Reminding myself that I was doing nothing wrong, I headed to the cosmetic aisle and looked around to make sure nobody was watching. *It's now or never.* I slipped my hand into my pocket and grabbed the nail polish, but just then somebody lurched toward me. I panicked and shoved the bottle back in my pocket before running out of the store.

I was only a few steps outside when someone called out. "Excuse me, young lady. Could you please come with me?" I turned around to see a man wearing a baseball cap and a pair of tinted glasses. My pounding heart popped out of my chest.

He escorted me to the back of the store and spoke to a woman wearing a name tag that only said "Manager." Before she could say anything, I reached into my pocket and pulled out the nail polish covered in sweat.

"Do you have a receipt for that?" she asked.

"Umm no. I swear I was just putting it back."

"You walked out of the store without paying for it. That's shoplifting." She shook her head while grabbing a piece of paper and pen. "I'm going to need the number of one of your parents."

Dad was at work and Mom was not here. I tapped my foot and the manager tapped hers. My fingers fidgeted in my pocket and I could feel something. *The origami fish with Poppy's mom's number.* I unfolded it and gave it to the manager. Without a word, she marched to the corner of the room and made a call. Her arms flapped but I couldn't hear anything.

It wasn't long before Poppy's mom arrived. After a quick exchange of words, they walked toward me. "Do you have something to say?" Poppy's mom's voice was calm and collected.

I turned toward the manager and apologized. "This will *never* happen again. I promise."

"I trust that it won't." She gave me an understanding nod, and I wondered what Poppy's mom said to her.

They shook hands. "Thank you again for not pressing charges." Poppy's mom gently placed her hand on my shoulder and walked me out.

The car ride home felt really long, probably because it was silent the whole time.

When the car pulled up in front of our house, I avoided any eye contact. "I'm sorry about all this."

"Emma, would you mind looking at me?"

I knew I was getting off too easy. I clenched my teeth and slowly turned to meet her gaze.

"Stealing is criminal."

Here it comes.

"But you know that, right?"

Huh?

"I can tell you have a good head on your shoulders."

I nodded in disbelief.

"You don't have to try so hard to be someone you're not."

Why is she so nice to me?

"You're great just the way you are."

I can't take it anymore!

"Mrs Sinclair . . ." My throat tightened. "That night you called me looking for Poppy, I lied to you."

I thought for sure she was going to get mad, tell me that I'm a bad friend, say that I was never allowed to hang out with Poppy again.

"Emma . . ." I closed my eyes. "I know."

"You know?" My head swivelled in her direction.

"After I talked to you that night, something didn't feel right, so I did my own investigation. Poppy was at a Halloween Party at Britannia Shipyards."

"How did you know?" I asked.

"I have my ways." She waved her phone as a smile formed on her face. In that moment I wasn't upset or scared for Poppy. I was envious of her.

"Does Poppy know that you know?"

"You learn to pick your battles. When she came home, I knew by her face that it wasn't time for a battle."

Poppy is so lucky.

"Poppy ended up telling me everything." She squeezed my hand. "So I know it wasn't your fault. You must have been put in such a tough spot."

My hand squeezed back, and I didn't want to let go.

When I got home, I could hear Dad's footsteps upstairs. I stayed downstairs and went to the kitchen. Everything was still left out. I preheated the oven and finished mixing in the juice. After making a trough in the dry ingredients, just like Poppy's mom taught me, I poured in the wet ingredients and a cup of dried cranberries. I gently folded the mixture before filling the pan.

While waiting for the muffins to bake, I kept rewinding what happened at the store. Things would have gone much smoother if I hadn't panicked. I could have returned what wasn't mine, and nobody would have known.

The timer rang and I pulled out the pan. I stared at the muffins. They could never become batter again. I guess some things just couldn't be undone—and maybe that was okay. I inhaled the smell of freshly baked muffins and thought of Poppy's mom.

CONDENSATION

A process in which a gas becomes a liquid.

I woke up with a pimple on my forehead, the first one I'd ever had. I ate more chocolates than ever and felt like a bloated balloon.

On the way to school, I walked through Garry Point and saw that the film crew was out again. The air felt damp, like it was about to rain. Suddenly a couple of spiky trolls rolled out from hiding, and a guy dressed in black jumped into a fighting stance. It reminded me of Olive, and I began thinking about what she'd said. Maybe she was right. I hadn't been myself lately. And what was I thinking? Olive would never tell on me. A raindrop fell on my head.

I was drenched by the time I got to school and went to the bathroom to dry myself. Olive stood in front of the mirror, sucking in her stomach and snivelling. As soon as she saw me, she zipped into a stall.

"Olive, I'm sorry for being a terrible friend." She flushed the toilet. The sound eventually dissipated. "You know I didn't mean what I said."

Her voice mumbled from inside the stall. "Yes you did.

They are more popular than me."

"It doesn't matter."

"It does to me."

I knew my words meant little to her at this point. I needed to do something to show her that I cared. Something I should have done earlier. "I won the contest for the meet and greet."

Silence.

"Don't you want the ticket?"

"Of course I do. But things are *not* okay between us."

"I entered the contest for *you.*"

"Did you really?"

"You're my best friend."

She came out of the stall with hurt smeared across her face. "Then why didn't you tell me about it sooner?"

I had no words to explain.

"It doesn't matter anyway. It's too late." She washed her face and left.

What do you mean?

I went to science but Olive wasn't there. She was right about a lot of things, including the cheating. *It isn't me.* As I contemplated coming clean, the zit on my forehead throbbed.

If I admitted what I had done, the others would also get in trouble. They'd be furious with me. If I didn't . . . I waited for Olive but she never came.

Mr Timberlac was acting stranger than usual, and class felt like it was taking forever. I listened to the simultaneous sound of the humming lights and ticking clock.

By the time science was finally over, I decided to admit the truth. The bell rang and I waited for everyone to leave the room. My mouth was dry but my hands were slick with sweat. As I made my way toward Mr Timberlac, I caught sight of Ivy through the doorway. She scowled at me and came into the classroom with Poppy and Suzy.

"What do you think you're doing?" Ivy muttered. Poppy and Suzy had the same concerned look. They motioned to me to follow them out of the room, and I took a step in their direction.

Mr Timberlac stood up and cleared his throat. "Did you want to tell me something?" He stared directly at me.

"Umm . . ." My eyes flitted between the ceiling and the ground.

"It's nothing," said Ivy.

Mr Timberlac squinted. "Lies are like gases in the atmosphere, often invisible, but sometimes they condense and the truth is revealed." He pulled out the crinkled cheat sheet.

I heard multiple gulps, like water going down a clogged drain. I had no choice but to say, "I wrote it."

Ivy looked like she was about to strangle me. Poppy turned pale and Suzy's eyes welled up.

"I'm the one who wrote the answers. It's not their fault."

Mr Timberlac rubbed his forehead. "You were all involved."

"Are you gonna fail us?" asked Poppy.

"Tell our parents?" cried Suzy.

"Can I go to the bathroom?" said Ivy.

He spun around on his chair with his fingers interlocked under his chin. Every time he completed a full rotation, my body tensed one more notch.

After what felt like an eternity, he halted. "I'll discuss this matter with your parents." Mr Timberlac stood up and left the classroom.

Poppy hung her head over her hand. Suzy was about to burst into tears. Ivy's lips devilishly curled as she turned toward Suzy. "Tell your parents the truth—that you're stupid and needed a boost."

Suzy's cheeks turned red like litmus paper in acid.

I frowned at Ivy.

"What?" She flicked her hair.

"This isn't a joke," Poppy said.

Ivy patted her back. "No biggie."

"No biggie?" Poppy flicked Ivy's hand off her back. "He could fail us or put it on our permanent records." She clasped her head and left.

"You just couldn't keep your mouth shut." Ivy glared at me with such toxicity that I wanted safety goggles to shield my eyeballs. "You truly are a dork!" Then she shoved my shoulder and stormed out.

Part of me wanted to blame Olive, but I knew deep down that none of this was her fault.

From the look on Dad's face, he didn't know why Mr Timberlac called a meeting. If anything, Dad acted as if he'd done something wrong. He had that same guilty look on his face as when he missed my science fair finals because he had to work late.

As we entered the school, Suzy was leaving, sandwiched between her parents. Her eyes were red and puffy. I tried to talk to her, but the expression on her mom's face warned me to leave her alone.

When we got to the classroom, Poppy and her mom were already there. I didn't have it in me to look at Poppy. Dad shook Mr Timberlac's hand before exchanging glances with Poppy's mom. The air was muggy with uncertainty.

"Hi, I'm Anne. You must be Hiro."

"Nice to meet you in person," Dad said.

In person. Had they already talked? Did Poppy's mom call Dad after the whole stealing incident? Why hadn't he mentioned anything?

Their gaze was interrupted by Mr Timberlac. "As I explained on the phone, your girls cheated on a test that makes up a significant portion of their term grade."

Dad knew? Why didn't he say anything on the way here?

"I don't understand. What would make Emma do something like this?" I looked at Dad but he wasn't asking me.

Even Mr Timberlac seemed to be coaxing Dad to look in my direction. "Emma's the one who gave her answers to the others." Then he stared directly at Poppy and me. "Cheating is a very serious offence."

My chest constricted. Both Poppy and her mom had worry written all over their faces, but Dad's was expressionless. *Why isn't he mad or upset?*

"Since neither of you have done this kind of thing before, I will not put this on your records."

Long breaths came out from Poppy and her mom, but not a twitch from Dad.

"However . . ." Mr Timberlac crossed his arms. "You must both write an essay on why you cheated. Since this is science class, I would like you to give me a scientific explanation."

My eyes finally met Poppy's. I couldn't tell what she was thinking, and it terrified me.

Our parents agreed that the punishment was suitable and thanked Mr Timberlac for his understanding.

As we made our way outside, Dad and Poppy's mom paused in the doorway and began talking. I slowly filled my lungs before I faced Poppy.

"I should never have asked you to do it . . . any of it," she said. Her eyes filled with regret, and I knew we were okay.

Our parents stepped out of the doorway. "Thanks again, Anne."

"Anytime, Hiro," said Poppy's mom before leaning in closer to me. "Emma, if you ever need to talk, I'm here for you." Her words hugged me tightly. Dad, on the other hand, was as silent as falling snow. Even on the car ride home, he wouldn't say a word.

"Did you hear what Mr Timberlac said? I cheated! Don't you care?"

"I . . . I don't understand, Emma." I could see his forehead wrinkle from the side. "What made you do it? Did something happen that I don't know about?"

"Lots has happened that we don't talk about. You don't pay attention to me anymore." As we turned into our neighbourhood, he pulled over and stopped the car. Finally we were going to talk.

"Why didn't you just come to me?"

"You've been different ever since you lost your job."

Dad went quiet again.

"Just admit it!" My words thundered. "You loved your old job, and you miss it. Admit it so you can move on with your life!"

He turned slowly toward me. I could feel we were on the brink of a breakthrough. "Emma." *Here it comes.* "It's not about work."

"Don't lie to me!"

He stared through the windshield, rubbing his forehead. "Dad?"

It was as if my voice popped his thought bubble. He shook his head and turned back to me. "I like what I'm doing now."

"Argh!" *Are you kidding?* "I can't talk to you!" I got out of the car and slammed the door. *What's happened to us?*

ELECTROSTATIC INTERACTIONS

Two oppositely charged particles attract one another.

When I woke up the next morning, I decided if Dad wasn't going to talk to me truthfully, then I had nothing to say to him. I walked right past his room even though I could hear him shuffling around in there.

My chocolate cravings were at an ultimate high, and I imagined a Gisele's Gelato announcement: "Our newest flavour is dairy-free chocolate ice cream."

I went to the kitchen to scrounge through Dad's chocolate stash. But all I found was a piece on the bottom shelf that, from the white coating on its surface, I knew was old. I ate it anyway.

My body felt heavy. I stretched out on the couch, letting my head slither off like a slug until I was upside down. A scientific reason for why I cheated? There was no reason, let alone a scientific one. I hadn't even wanted to. *Why did I do it?*

I started analyzing the string of events that had occurred. I'd done a bunch of things I regretted, but given another chance I think I still would have done the same things. I didn't want to be left out—I wanted to fit in. I swung my legs back down and wrote out some notes.

"Peer pressure is real. It makes you do things even though you know they are wrong." I crossed it out and wrote a new opening line. *"High school is hard, even if you're popular. When you're not, it's even worse."*

Maybe I'll just blame it on teenage hormones.

"Hormones are special chemical messengers in the body. They control bodily functions such as hunger and mood. They also control behaviour, especially in teens."

I went to Dad's computer and searched the keywords hormones, adolescents and behaviours. One article talked about the importance of peer acceptance to succeed in school. For me it was never about the grades, but I was comforted to know that it was normal to care what others thought.

Another one talked about the brain hormone oxytocin, and how it's related to the feeling of belonging. The article referred to it as the "love hormone" because it gives you those gushy feelings when you cuddle with someone you love. "Oxytocin is released when you bond deeply with others," I read aloud. "It strengthens relationships, even on a social level."

That's it! I continued to write. *"I was involved in cheating because I wanted to feel accepted. I wanted a stronger bond with my peers. A sense of belonging is induced when your body releases oxytocin. Therefore I was encouraging my brain to release oxytocin."*

Speaking of hormones and bodily changes, I was definitely going through something. My face was oilier than usual, my stomach felt like I'd eaten a bucket of dairy, and my boobs were super tender—like they were growing. *Where's Mom?* I checked my email again but she still hadn't replied.

After I finished my essay and emailed it to Mr Timberlac, I thought I would feel better. If anything, I felt worse. *I could use a good dose of oxytocin—a hormone that makes you feel good and strengthens relationships.* My relationships could definitely use some strengthening. I thought back to what Ms Grimaldi had said about forming a real connection.

How do two people form a real connection . . . a bond?

How does a chemical bond form?

Dad came into his office. His mouth opened. "Um . . ."

"Yes?"

"How's your essay going?"

"I'm done."

"That's great." He grinned before his face turned more serious. "I . . . there's something . . ." He fumbled and knocked over a bunch of papers. When he crouched down to pick them up, I saw a sock clinging to the back of his sweater vest. An idea sparked—*negative and positive charges attract.* "Opposites attract!" I yelled.

Dad looked puzzled, but I had no time to explain. I ran back to my room and began writing down my final advice to Poppy. I scribbled some stuff about static electricity and electrostatic interactions, then added, *"Hence there is a scientific basis for the saying, opposites attract."*

Examples in film came to mind: an ugly creature who catches the heart of a beautiful soul, a poor protagonist who ends up marrying a rich royal, a fragile main character who finds comfort in a gigantic protector. I even thought about Mom and Dad. Dad an introvert, Mom an extrovert; Dad was disorganized, Mom was tidy; Dad a nerd, Mom a fashionista; clumsy Dad, elegant Mom; Dad showed signs of balding, Mom had gorgeous hair. I could go on and on. They were as opposite as could be, the reason they got together in the first place.

It totally made sense from a practical standpoint too. *"If the two of you are different, you'll be more interesting to each other. You'll have more to talk about and more to learn. And any disputes could spark some thought-provoking debates."*

Next I thought of a real-life situation: *"Let's say you're sharing a bag of mixed popcorn with both cheddar and caramel flavours. If one person likes savoury and the other person likes sweet, you both get what you want. You're both satisfied."*

Both scientific and practical. *"Thus, the more opposite you are, the more sparks you'll have."*

I closed my notebook and headed to Poppy's house. As I walked through Garry Point, a lady with a long overcoat stood in the field staring at the sky. I soon realized it was Ms Grimaldi. She wasn't wearing her usual glasses, and her hair was down, but it was still as neat as a pin.

"Hi, Ms Grimaldi. What are you looking at?"

She pointed to an orange octopus swerving in the air. "My boyfriend's flying that kite." On the other end was a guy, unwinding the string. When I caught a glimpse of his face, I was stunned.

Mr Timberlac?

I quickly waved goodbye to them and dashed away. The last thing I needed was for Mr Timberlac to bring up my essay or the whole cheating fiasco.

But I was glad to run into them. My orderly English teacher with my chaotic science teacher only confirmed the principle that opposites attract.

I was almost at Poppy's but had to slow down. I felt as if someone was wringing out my stomach from inside. The pain was unlike anything I'd felt before.

When I finally got to Poppy's house, her mom answered the door. I wanted to hug her and thank her again for being there for me, but I didn't know if that would be weird. Then she hugged me and everything felt okay. Except my stomach. I held it and let out a groan.

"Are you okay?" she asked with concern in her voice.

"I have a stomach ache." Poppy's mom gave me some tea and a hot water bottle to place on my tummy. It still hurt but they helped.

Poppy was in her room, hunched over and swiping her phone. Her hair was frazzled and so was she. She looked how I felt.

"What's wrong?" I asked.

"For one, I have no idea what to write in this essay for Mr Timberlac. I'm pulling out my hair thinking about it." Then she showed me a picture of herself holding a slice of pizza in one hand and a cup of tea in the other. "I just read an interview with Cole. It mentions that his favourite food is pizza and he likes drinking tea. But he hasn't liked my picture." She slumped onto her bed. "I'm getting nowhere, and the meet and greet's in like a week."

"Instead of liking the same things he does, try liking the opposite," I said. "It makes you more interesting."

"But what's the opposite of pizza . . . or tea?"

I shrugged and gave her my notes. She crinkled her nose as she read them. "How do I make sure I'm his opposite if I don't *really* know him?"

My first thought was *Why would you like someone you don't really know?* She was back on her phone, thumbing through Cole's pictures. "I can't tell what he likes from these."

I offered to find out for her. "I'll ask Cole so you can be prepared." All of a sudden my stomach creaked like an old floor, and I bent over. Poppy gave me a peculiar look, and I started babbling. "I'm lactose intolerant. I've been eating a lot of chocolate, mainly milk chocolate, so my stomach's a little sore."

I held my tummy and excused myself to the bathroom. Sitting on the toilet seat, I closed my eyes. When I opened them I saw something I wasn't ready for. A reddish, brownish smudge. Oh no. I felt dizzy. *Blood is just made of blood cells. They're like any other cell—muscle cell, nerve cell, skin cell, stem cell.* It wasn't helping.

Everything was turning white with blue outlines. I was fainting, and there was nothing I could do about it.

Next thing I knew, I was lying on a bed with both Poppy and her mom by my side. When I realized what had happened, I propped myself up. "I think I got my . . ." I still couldn't say the word.

"Period." Poppy finished my sentence. "We figured. You have a zit—the first one I've ever seen on your face—you've been binging on chocolates more than normal, and you have cramps."

Poppy's mom placed her hand on my back. "It's perfectly normal." They smiled at each other before looking my way, like they were welcoming me into a new club.

COMBUSTION

A rapid chemical reaction in the presence of oxygen that gives off heat.

With the meet and greet less than a week away, I needed to get more information on Cole so Poppy could implement the opposites attract plan. But first I needed something else. I went to Mom's powder room to find some feminine products. As I checked the cupboards, I heard Dad and quickly hid behind the door. *How awkward would that be?* I wished Mom were here. *She should be here.* I slammed shut the cupboard door, not finding anything. When I turned toward the mirror, I saw that the zit on my forehead had exploded.

Remembering that Mom had some foundation, I went to her vanity and patted a bit of it onto my forehead with a sponge. I remembered Mom not so long ago sitting in front of her mirror applying blush to her cheeks. I asked her if I could try some, and she softly tapped my nose with her brush. "I'll teach you about makeup . . . when you become a teenager."

It all made sense now. My birthday was two days after Christmas, which, according to Mom, was a time to cherish

with family. She'd be home in time to wear her favourite heels to Dad's holiday party, and she'd get me makeup for my thirteenth birthday. She'd be home soon!

She can't come home to this mess. I pulled out the vacuum and sucked up all the dust bunnies. I collected the dishes and washed them. I placed all the loose pieces from Dad's molecular model set and the tiles from Elementabble back in their designated boxes. Next I went to clean the main bathroom and even found some maxi pads. Finally I went to my room, put all my knick-knacks back where they belonged and folded my clothes into their drawers. My experimental plants were dying, but I couldn't quite bring myself to throw them out, so I pushed them to the other side of the window sill, wiped the ledge clean and finished tidying up.

Now that our place looked decent enough for Mom to come home to, I could focus on Poppy and Cole.

As I didn't have Cole's number, I called George's house.

Unfortunately, George picked up, so I got straight to the point. "Where's Cole?"

"He's filming at Garry Point."

I started to hang up.

"Wait! I'm sorry I gave you bogus advice. A girl like Poppy doesn't like guys like me. I thought by helping you I could . . ."

"Get her to like you?" I shook my head. "You can't force someone to like you."

"Isn't that what you're doing?"

"It's completely different." I wasn't forcing anyone to like me. Or was I? I changed the subject. "I heard the story you made up about the mouse chasing Cole. Nice thinking." I couldn't help giggling.

"Emma, I really never meant to hurt you." His voice was tainted with regret. "I guess I was desperate."

I understood exactly how he felt.

I arrived at Garry Point to see several goblins scampering across the field to hide under a fort. Cole and the others ran after them dressed in cloaks. All of a sudden, *bang!*—a huge explosion. As soon as the director called "Cut," I looked for Cole to make sure he was okay.

When I saw him, my heart skipped a beat. I ignored it and waved to him.

"You're finally talking to me?" he said.

"What do you mean?"

"You've been avoiding me."

Kinda. "Sorry, I've just been really busy."

"It's okay, I'll forgive you." His smile put me at ease.

"Can I ask you a few random questions?"

He rubbed his hands and blew into them. "Sure, but it's freezing. Let's go get a hot drink."

We ended up at Maritime Anytime. He got a chamomile tea, and I got a hot cocoa made with coconut milk. We made our way to a table with an anchor painted on it. "What did you want to ask me?"

Tell me everything about you so I can tell Poppy. "Do you like apples or oranges?"

"Apples. You?"

"Oranges. They're juicier and more flavourful."

"But you get more variety with apples," he said.

"Good point. But oranges contain more vitamins and minerals."

"Aren't we just comparing apples to oranges?"

I almost snickered but stopped myself. I had to stay on task. "Next question: are you an early bird or a night owl?"

"Night owl. It's more peaceful in the evenings. It's when I do most of my thinking. You?"

"Early bird. The early mornings are quiet too. Plus, morning people tend to be healthier. The deep restorative sleep, also known as non-rapid eye movement, dominates your sleep cycle in the early part of the night."

He didn't argue that one.

"Next question: cats or dogs?"

"Cats! They're smarter," he answered.

"Actually, dogs possess approximately 530 million neurons

in the cerebral cortex while cats have less than half of that, around 250 million."

"You really are different." He smirked. "But in a good way."

I felt a spark.

Wait a minute . . .

Our answers were all opposites.

Plus he's tall, I'm short; he likes savoury, I like sweet; he's an actor, I'm a scientist. Nope, nope, nope . . . I can't. Poppy likes Cole.

My mind spun like a magnetic stirrer on high speed. I had to get Poppy and Cole together. And fast.

I stood up.

He stood up.

He stared into my eyes. "I want to tell you something." My heart beat like a taiko drum. "I really like you, Emma."

This can't be happening. I quickly grabbed my notebook and the rest of my stuff. In a panic, I tripped. Cole reached out his arms, and I fell into them.

Someone shrieked at a super-high frequency. I turned around to see Poppy with her mouth hanging open. I jumped as far away from Cole as possible. "It's not what it looks like."

"How could you?" Her lips trembled and her face burned bright. She was about to explode.

"I can explain."

She bolted out before I could say another word.

Cole looked completely and utterly confused. How was I supposed to explain? I ran out, hoping this was all a bad dream.

BLACK HOLE

A black hole is a region of space exhibiting such a strong gravitational pull that nothing can escape from it.

I couldn't fall asleep that night, so I wasn't able to wake up from this nightmare. Flashbacks of Poppy's raging face kept racing through my mind.

Where are you, Mom? I need you! Why hadn't she called me or at least replied to my email? She'd said "See you soon" when she left, but it was way past that now. Why would she lie? Even though hope was slipping away, I checked to see if she'd messaged me back. Heart beating, I opened my inbox.

There it was.

"Dear Emma,"

In that moment I forgot everything else.

"Sorry we haven't had a chance to talk in a while. Regarding your question, tell your friend to not do anything." Huh? *"Don't change yourself for a guy or for anyone. If you can't be yourself, it'll never work out in the long run. I miss you so very much and think of you often. A lot has been going on. I'll explain everything when I can.*

Love, Mom"

My heart burst with relief. I knew she missed me.

"*Dear Mom,*

Thanks for your advice! It makes total sense." I wanted to go on and on about everything that had been happening but decided to tell her in person. The holidays were right around the corner and she'd be home. "*Can't wait to see you! Missing you too!*

Love, Emma"

Send.

Mom's advice really made me think. *Be yourself.* I wasn't being honest with Poppy. I knew I had to tell her the whole truth, hoping she'd understand. I started typing an email but stopped. I'd read that a handwritten note was much more meaningful and brought out my C Ho Co La Te notebook. I wrote a letter to Poppy explaining everything as best as I could from beginning to end.

Poppy stood at her locker with a book that showed a vase on the cover. Just as I took a step toward her, Ivy and Suzy swooped in. I hesitated but took another step. *She just needs to read the letter.*

Poppy's eyes were so furious they looked flammable. "How could you! I gave you fashion tips like we agreed, even gave you clothes." She threw up her hands. "You ruined everything! *You* liked Cole all along and sabotaged me. I can't believe I dressed as stinky cheese. I can't believe I ever trusted you!"

"Please just look at this." I extended my arm with the letter. Poppy grabbed it, stared right into my eyes and shredded the pages into pieces. "I actually thought you were my friend."

"I told you she's a loser," Ivy boasted.

Suzy didn't say anything, but she wouldn't look at me either.

Poppy flicked her hair. "Let's go. She's not worth our time."

My heart ripped into shreds like the letter.

I ran to the washroom, into the farthest stall, holding back my tears. Every time a whimper crept out, I flushed the toilet.

Why did I have to lie about everything—even about Mom? *I don't even know where she is.*

I started to panic like I was trapped. I searched for an article to read but couldn't find one. Suddenly I heard footsteps and peeked through a crack. Olive stood in front of the mirror fixing her hair. I could see her eyes through her reflection, and all I wanted to do was hug her.

Even though I was sure she'd leave, I unlocked the door and came out.

"Emma, what's wrong?"

I couldn't hold it in anymore and burst out crying. Olive just embraced me.

Finally I calmed.

"I'm sorry I gave the cheat sheet to Mr Timberlac."

"I don't care about that. What if my mom doesn't come home?"

"You'll be fine," she said in a soothing voice.

"How do you know?"

"'Cause you're the strongest person I know."

I looked at her for forgiveness. "I'm so sorry, Olive, for everything. Can we start over?"

"You let me down so many times."

"I won't let you down again."

"How do I know?"

"I really miss you!"

"I've missed you too." I knew she meant it.

"Take my winning ticket. Have fun at the meet and greet."

She paused before holding my wrist with the DNA bracelet. "Look, I really hope everything works out with you and your mom, but . . . I can't just forget everything that's happened between us." She let go and my arm swung down like a wrecking ball. Olive had a piece of my heart. I only felt it when she took it away.

I ran outside as fast as I could, letting the wind dry my tears. I darted through the school field and a pathway to the back road. *What if Mom never comes home?* I'd never said those words before. I felt like she was leaving all over again. A car honked and I leapt back on the sidewalk, feeling more lost than ever. *I'm a terrible person. No wonder everyone leaves me.* The wind blew fiercely, and the memory that I'd been suppressing so tightly surged into my mind.

EVAPORATION

The process in which a liquid becomes a gas.

Our cherry tree was in full bloom that day. I'd been looking out the window, listening to the whispers of the wind, when I heard yelling. I ran out to the hallway to see Mom and Dad. They quickly slipped into their room.

I cuffed my ear to their door. "It's not working," said Mom.

Silence.

"I miss how we used to be," said Dad.

"Me too."

How they used to be. I ran to the kitchen and put on the kettle. I took out two of Mom's finest teacups and placed some chocolate-covered biscuits on a plate that was only used on special occasions.

I suddenly heard a door slam so hard the walls shook. Their voices were now coming from outside. Mom walked toward the cherry tree and Dad trailed behind. Blossoms fell like snowflakes in the strong wind, and I couldn't see much except their arms flailing. Then Dad's arms shot up. "So what, you're just going to leave?"

I sprinted into their room. A suitcase filled with clothes and shoes—Mom's favourite gold heels on top—sat open on her side of the bed.

With heels in hand, I hurried to the kitchen. Steam rose from the kettle. I peeked outside to see that they were still at it, then quickly gathered what I needed in a pot: water, corn syrup and a splash of white vinegar, and heated it on the stove. As soon as the mixture came to a boil, I took it off the heat and added it to a bowl of cornstarch and ice-cold water.

I threw the heels into the freezer and poured the glue-like concoction on top. "There," I said, dusting my hands. "Mom's never gonna leave without them."

Several minutes later the door opened. Mom came in and ran upstairs. *She'll wonder where her heels went. She'll search everywhere and will have to come ask me.*

Dad came into the kitchen with dark bags under his eyes.

I handed him some tea. "What's happening?"

"Not now, Emma."

"Where's Mom going?"

He rubbed his eyes. "She'll keep us informed."

"Dad, I don't get it."

"Everything will be fine." His voice was not convincing. "I already found a new job." He grabbed a chocolate-covered biscuit but just fiddled with it.

Mom never came to ask me about her heels. I went to knock on her door but stopped when I heard her voice. "So you'll pick me up?"

The knot in my chest strained as I opened the door. "You're really leaving?"

Her face said it all and her suitcase was closed. *Does she not care about her heels? She loves them.* Pain shot through me. "Why, Mom?"

She paused. "It's hard to explain."

"Where are you going? When are you coming back?"

"I just need some time. I'll let you know as soon as I figure things out." She touched her forehead to mine and let it rest there as she said a few more words.

What? Why? Where? I couldn't understand.

The next thing I knew, Mom pulled away. A beam of light flashed through the window, and I jumped up to look out. An expensive-looking car with a logo similar to a peace sign had pulled up in our driveway.

I heard a suitcase rolling down the hallway. *No!* I whipped around and chased the sound. The sweet smell of Mom's perfume lingered.

She stopped in front of the door.

Her hair veiled her face so I couldn't see it.

She must be thinking.

She knows she's making a big mistake.

She's going to turn around.

Then she did, toward me. I saw a flicker of hesitation.

"Mom?"

"See you soon, Emma." She gazed down, opened the door and walked out.

I couldn't move.

By the time I went outside, the driveway was empty and so was the street.

Mom was gone. She had evaporated along with the smell of her perfume.

See you soon, Emma.

That was eight months ago.

CHAPTER 33

CRYSTALLIZATION

A process in which highly structured crystals are formed.

My legs carried me all the way to the dock, and I realized I had completely ditched school. Thinking about Olive and Poppy and what I had done to them made me nauseous. My head was spinning, but for the first time I saw with crystal clarity: *Mom may never come home.* The colours faded around me like a sun-bleached painting. *What am I going to do?* If my own mom couldn't love me, how could anyone else? A chill went up my spine, and I was as numb as snow.

I didn't go to school the next day. Dad knocked on my door, but I told him to go away. A few minutes later he knocked again and slid something under the door.

After an unknown time of staring at the ceiling, I saw that he'd left me a chocolate bar. I rolled over in my bed until I heard another knock. This time the door cracked open, and the smell of something sweet and familiar wafted in. I waited until the door closed before looking at what it

was: a stack of Dad's famous hotcakes with a side of maple syrup in an Erlenmeyer flask.

I got up and took a bite. Slowly I started to feel something again. I quickly went back to bed, pulled the blanket over myself and fell asleep until . . .

"Emma." I covered my head with my pillow. "I have something to show you."

I threw my covers over my pillow-smothered head.

"Get up. I promise it'll be worth your while." There was a liveliness to his voice that I hadn't heard in a long time.

Lifting the corner of the blanket, I peeked out. Dad wore a lab coat and safety goggles with a smile across his face. Curious, I started to get up. He told me to meet him in the kitchen and ran down before I got there.

Smoke filled the room, but it didn't smell like something had burned. Dad held a dewar of liquid nitrogen, pouring it into a metal bowl and stirring it like he was concocting a potion.

Not even a minute later he handed me a beaker mug. "Dairy-free chocolate ice cream," he said.

I grabbed it and took a spoonful. For a moment I let myself forget everything that had happened. Dad scooped himself a bowl, and we sat there in silence. We looked at each other candidly, like we used to, and the sheet of ice between us began to thaw.

As my last bite melted away, reality stung me. I couldn't hold it in any longer. "Is she coming home?" My voice shook.

He put down his bowl and stared out like he always did when he was avoiding something. Any warmth he'd given me was dissipating by the second. "Dad, please tell me the truth."

Something in his face changed. His eyebrows sagged and his lips stiffened. I could hear his breath as he exhaled. "Your mom and I are separating. She's not coming home."

My body heated up and cooled almost simultaneously, like pain and relief all at once. "Why didn't you tell me?"

"I didn't know how."

"So you're giving up?"

"Giving up is *never* the answer." He said it like he believed it.

"So you're going to fight for it, right?"

"Unfortunately by the time I figured out what to fight for, it was too late."

"If I'd known what was happening, I could have helped."

"We didn't want you to worry about our problems."

"But if it was between the two of you, why would she leave me?" My body began to quiver. "Why did Mom say 'See you soon'? Why not the truth?" I knocked my elbow on the counter and started bawling.

Dad rubbed my back. "Things don't always work out, even when we really want them to." He waited until I stopped crying. "We both thought it was best for you to stay here with me, your friends, your home. She wants you to visit once she's settled."

"Was she ever going to tell me? Say goodbye?"

His face strained and tears welled up in his eyes. "How could anybody say goodbye to you?"

"I miss her so much!" Tears flooded out again.

He handed me a tissue and grabbed one for himself. "I miss her too." He wiped his tears before looking in my direction. "But you're my silver lining."

That's when I realized that Dad had the same cloud of gloom as me. "So you weren't sad about losing your job?"

He shook his head. "I'd had so much admin work, it took away from my love of science, not to mention that I was barely around."

He really wasn't home much before.

"I feel like I'm making a real difference now. And the best part: I get to spend more quality time with you."

"Quality?" I arched a brow.

"I admit I've been out of it. But I'll make more quality time." We hugged tightly, and I knew he meant it.

As we let go of each other, I said, "If you really want to spend quality time with me, I probably shouldn't go to school . . . for the rest of the year."

"Do you want to talk about it?"

"Not really." Everyone hated me, and there was nothing I could do or say to fix that.

"So you're giving up?"

"Ha ha, Dad. Giving up is *never* the answer." I said it exactly the way he'd said it to me. But by uttering those words, I realized one difference between us.

It wasn't too late for me. I still had the winning ticket for the meet and greet.

CELL THEORY

All living things are composed of one or more cell(s).

When I got to science class, I looked for an empty seat with my eyes on the floor. It was hard to ignore the giant gift box topped with a ribbon at the front of the classroom. I heard a couple of girls complaining that Cole still wasn't in class because he was wrapping up filming. When I looked up momentarily, I saw Olive standing by Poppy's desk. My insides crumpled as I imagined what they were talking about—how I'm the worst friend ever.

The bell rang, and suddenly Mr Timberlac popped out of the box. "Surprise!" He looked like a game show host wearing a blazer and necktie. "Hope you did your reading assignment. We're having a pop quiz today." There was clamour among the class. Only Mr Timberlac would give us a test right before the holidays.

Proceeding to an empty seat, I tripped and hit the floor. I recognized Ivy's purple-soled shoe by my face. She slid her foot back under her chair, and I got up to see her covering her mouth, but the edges of her smile poked out.

"Are you alright?" asked Mr Timberlac.

"I'm fine." Every cell in my body told me to stand up for myself. Instead I pressed my lips together and proceeded to my seat. How was I going to get through class . . . the rest of the year . . . the rest of high school? I looked over the quiz questions.

Question 1: What do all human cells contain?
a. DNA
b. ribosomes
c. cytoplasm
d. all of the above

Maybe I could transfer? Maybe I could homeschool myself? I rested my face on my palm.

"Ahem!" Mr Timberlac stared down at me. "Is there a problem?"

I shook my head, looked at my paper and answered the question: d, all of the above. Mr Timberlac paced up and down my aisle, which forced me to focus on the test.

Question 2: Which of the following is a basic principle of cell theory?
a. all organisms are composed of cells
b. the cell is a basic unit of structure in all living things
c. cells originate from pre-existing cells
d. all of the above

I circled d, then thought about everyone as cell types again: stem, muscle, bone, skin, nerve—all so different, yet so similar. Too bad our differences stuck out more in high school.

After school, groups of people lingered around the main foyer, talking. I weaved through the crowds, avoiding any contact, but I couldn't help overhearing some of the conversations. Coding guy, Raymond, and breakdancing guy, Zach, chatted about a new dance app that just came out. Gum guy, Peter, and hair guy, Mike, talked about their upcoming ski trips to Whistler during the holidays. Head-bopper, Chase, wore wireless earphones, jiving to his tunes.

Surprisingly, George was speaking with Poppy. She said something to him about the *Magical Creatures* meet and greet, with concern on her face. George said something back to her that I couldn't quite make out, but whatever he said made her giggle.

I overheard Olive, Molly and Holly also talking about the meet and greet. "They're making the winner's name public today before the live show," said Molly.

"Do you think it's someone from our school?" asked Holly.

I thought for sure Olive would give me away. "Wouldn't we already know if they were?"

Ivy approached them from the other side with Suzy, and said, "Well good thing it wasn't you, Olive oil. Have you looked in the mirror lately?" Suzy tugged on Ivy's arm but she wouldn't stop. "You'd look like a balloon."

Olive's face turned crimson. Her lips quivered but no words came out.

Actions speak louder than words. I took a deep breath, squared my shoulders and marched over. "Ivy, why do you act like this?" Everyone nearby glanced in our direction. "Olive never did anything to you, except to defend me."

Ivy raised her upper lip. "This, coming from an even bigger loser."

I wanted to look down, but I held my head high and stared her right in the eyes. "Look, Ivy. I know you're going through some stuff of your own, but just because you're unhappy with yourself, you don't have to take it out on us."

Ivy looked flabbergasted. She grasped Suzy's arm. "Let's not waste our time."

Suzy pulled away. "Actually I think I'll stay right here."

"What?" Ivy sneered. "You'd rather stick around with these dweebs?"

"They're not dweebs, losers or geeks. They're just good friends," Suzy exclaimed. "Something I can't say about you."

Ivy was tongue-tied for the first time. But it didn't last. "Whatever!" She flicked her hair and stamped away.

"That's cool the way you stuck up for Olive, and for calling Ivy out." Suzy gave me a friendly nod before walking in the opposite direction of Ivy.

I turned to Olive. "I don't expect you to forgive me, but I still want you to have the ticket."

"I told you, I'm not taking it."

"Look, you don't have to be friends with me, but it's yours. I'll be at the studio early to get the name transferred. It's your choice to meet me there."

"Okay," she replied with a half-smile.

On the way home I ran into Cole. A strange mix of emotions ran over me. "Sorry I just took off the other day."

I could tell he was waiting for an explanation. As I gazed into his eyes, I couldn't stand the thought of lying to him anymore. I told him everything, from the agreement Poppy and I made to all the lies I'd been telling just to keep up the charade.

A long pause.

Out of nowhere, he laughed out loud. "That explains the cheese chasing me." Then his smile turned upside down. "Is that why you were asking me so many questions?"

"Yes. But Cole, I started to feel something."

"The same feelings I have for you?"

I rubbed the back of my neck. "The truth is, I don't really know. So much has been going on." I peered away before looking back at him. "The one thing I don't regret is that I got to know you." I held out my hand. "I hope we can still be friends."

A short pause.

"The truth is," he said and accepted my hand, "I could really use a friend."

Letting the air breeze over me, I gazed into the harbour and began thinking. Everybody was more alike than I had thought. It didn't really matter what cell type we most resembled. At the end of the day, we were all made up of the same things . . . and we each had our own struggles.

The sun shone brightly but the air was icy cold. "Books!" I turned around to see Poppy. "You won?"

They must have made the name public. "I did."

"I'm so excited. The host of VTVZ, Cargo Davies, is gonna be there to interview the cast with the winner." She gazed skyward. "He's got over a *million* followers. Can you believe it?"

I swallowed a lump. "I already told Olive she could have it."

"Oh, right." She scratched her head. "Is it because you thought I was mad at you? 'Cause I'm not. George explained everything. That you really were trying to help me. He admitted that he purposely fed you bad advice because he liked me." She placed her palm over her chest. "Nobody's ever done anything like that for me."

I was speechless.

"Now that we're friends again, I'll happily accept the winning ticket. I don't know if you need to be there to transfer names, but better meet me at the studio, just in case. I'm gonna get my hair and makeup done beforehand."

My mouth dropped open. *Say something.* "I really did . . ."

"It'll actually be a good distraction. My parents have been acting weird lately. My mom rented a cabin for a few days during the holidays so we could spend some quality, uninterrupted "girl time" together, to bake chocolate chip cookies, do our nails, all that fun stuff. I could ask my mom if you could come."

"Poppy . . ."

"Whatever it is, save it for the show! I have so much to do to get ready!" She took off before I could say another word.

MELTING POINT

The temperature at which a solid becomes a liquid.

At the VTVZ studio, I was met by a friendly man who congratulated me on winning the ticket. Down the hall, lit by bright lights and neon signs, a lady with a headset was talking to Cole. He waved at me before turning down a narrow corridor.

Shortly after, Poppy strutted in wearing a fitted dress suit and retro flats, looking more glamorous than ever. She held up her phone immediately and snapped a few photos of the surroundings before turning the camera around and craning her neck toward the VTVZ logo.

I hurried toward her. "I have to tell you something."

"I know. My lips could use a little zing." She applied some lip gloss. "Let's get a photo together." She put her arm around me.

Just then Olive came running in with tousled hair, huffing and puffing. My eyes flickered between the two.

The lady with the headset came over. "Emma Sakamoto, could you come with me?"

"Wait," I said. "I'm giving my ticket to my friend." Poppy smiled so hard even her dimples looked excited.

The lady shrugged her shoulders with her palms up. "Which friend?"

Poppy scrunched her nose, bit her lip, then gave me a peculiar look. "Did I tell you I asked my mom, and she said you're welcome to come with us to the cabin, you know, to spend some quality girl time with us?"

A wave of hurt came crashing down Olive's face.

I inhaled. "Poppy." And exhaled slowly. "I'm sorry, but I've already given my ticket to Olive. I tried to tell you."

"I got you a sample of this new lip gloss . . ." Poppy's voice trailed off. Her eyebrows pinched together, then she blinked several times. Her face flushed, like she was embarrassed. Then she turned a different shade of red, like she was mad. Her eyes seared, then simmered, then cooled. It was as if she were undergoing a chemical reaction. Her face softened as she looked toward Olive. "I understand."

In a hazy but crazy moment, Poppy opened her purse, took out a brush and swept the hair off Olive's face. She pulled out a makeup kit and went to apply some blush.

"Thanks but I'm good. I have naturally rosy cheeks." Olive hugged her grinning face with both hands before skipping toward the stage.

I turned to Poppy. "I really did try to tell you."

"I know. I just didn't want to hear it," she admitted. "I wanted us to have what you and Olive have."

I was lost for words.

"You know, Olive came up to me when I was still mad at you and told me to give you a break—that you've been

through a lot." Poppy's phone dinged but she ignored it. "Not to mention that George felt so bad for what he did to you, he would have done anything to make it up to you. You're really lucky to have such good friends. Made me think about what I've been missing."

It was true. Olive and George were friends that I could totally be myself around. I realized then that fitting in was not the same thing as belonging. I couldn't be myself when I was trying to fit in, but all I had to do was be myself to belong. "So you're not upset about Cole?"

"Obviously I'm a little bummed that it didn't work out. But it's my first high school crush. I'll get over it." Then she started snickering. "Still can't believe you said you wrote a book about the *science of boys*. You're as clueless as I am."

"Totally clueless." We laughed so hard I could feel it in my belly.

After the show, Olive came running off the stage. "That was the best experience of my life! Thanks, Emma!"

"It's the least I can do."

"It wasn't entirely your fault." Olive puckered her lips. "I was jealous and wanted us to get back to the way things were." She lifted up her wrist with the DNA bracelet back on. I clinked it with mine.

When we left the studio, a snowflake landed on my nose. By the time the bus got us back to Steveston, the ground looked as if it were sprinkled with icing sugar. We said our goodbyes. Olive squeezed me tightly, and Poppy gave me an equally big squeeze. Then Poppy and Olive hugged.

Festive lights and decorations beamed from every house in our neighbourhood. Even from ours. *Dad decorated!* Icicles dangled from our roof, and fairies from *Magical Creatures* frolicked on our porch with Santa hats.

I went inside to see a bunch of boxes. I knew they weren't from the Christmas decorations—Mom's scarf draped out from one of them.

The knot forming in my chest loosened when I saw that Dad had set up a game of Elementabble. He'd already made the first move, Ca N Dy, with calcium, nitrogen, dysprosium.

His voice echoed from the kitchen. "Make your move. I'll be right there."

I added fluorine and uranium to his nitrogen to make F U N.

He brought out a plate of chocolate-covered biscuits and hot cocoa with dollops of non-dairy whipped cream. Then he made his next move, F La K Es, with fluorine, lanthanum, potassium, einsteinium. I could tell by the way he spoke that he was pleased with himself.

"Sulfur, nitrogen, oxygen, tungsten." I placed S N O W in front of his word. "Snowflakes, triple letter score for W."

He gave me a proud look then placed two tiles in front of me: Lu, lutetium, and V, vanadium.

"Lu V? That's not a real word," I said.

"It is for me." He leaned in and kissed my forehead.

We finished our game and I went to the kitchen, knowing what I had to do. The temperature was perfect outside. I removed the contents from inside the fridge and freezer and carried them outside, placing them on a layer of snow. Then I unplugged the fridge.

After all the ice had melted, I opened the freezer door. The sticky goo remained on Mom's gold heels, but I yanked them out and washed them.

When they dried, I placed them in a box to return to Mom.

CHAPTER 36

PHOTOSYNTHESIS

A natural process by which plants use water and sunlight to make food for themselves in order to grow.

water + light + carbon dioxide →glucose + oxygen

The snow quickly melted with the rain. Just as quickly, the rain ceased and the clouds vanished. Trees revealed their evergreen, houses showed off their distinct hues, and the sky gleamed blue. I noticed that I didn't have to try so hard to breathe.

Olive was supposed to pick me up to go to Gisele's, but she was late again. I slipped on my comfy green jacket and waited in my room, flipping through an issue of *Science Today and Tomorrow*. I stopped when I saw a figure of some lively plants. To the side was a text bubble that read "Plants require both water and light to grow." I got up to check on my own experimental plants, which were doing much better. It turned out that when I was cleaning and pushed the plants to the other side of the window, they got more sunlight.

Olive finally showed up wearing a golden-yellow shirt. We clinked our wrists and walked to Gisele's.

"No more black outfits?" I asked.

"Yellow hues are supposed to complement my skin tone."

"I read a study on how the colour we wear impacts our mood and behaviour."

She smiled and tugged on my jacket. "Speaking of, that colour looks great on you."

"Thanks, my dad got it for me for my birthday."

"Oh, right." Olive turned away.

"Don't worry if you forgot. There was so much going on this year."

We got to the entrance of Gisele's. Olive halted and started fiddling with her bracelet. "Can you open the door?"

"Did your bracelet break off?"

"It's fine. Just open the door."

"Surprise!" An ensemble of voices erupted.

Standing there were Poppy, George, Cole, Molly, Holly and Suzy. A sign hung above them: HAPPY BIRTHDAY, EMMA! They hugged me one by one, and I felt the warmth from each one of them. We all squeezed into a booth and ate gelato, talking about all sorts of stuff. We laughed a lot and even cried a little. We were just ourselves, and it felt really good.

Every so often my cloud returns, but I don't mind it as much anymore. How can you grow without a little rain?

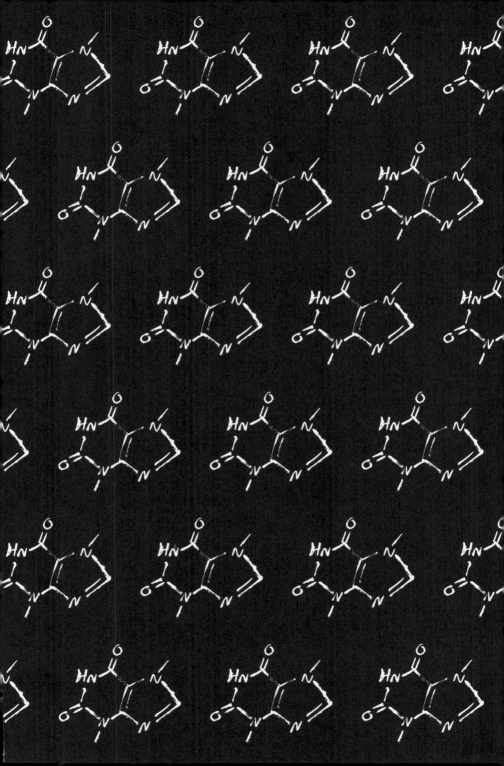

ACKNOWLEDGEMENTS

To my school friends, Christina Kent, Kristy Vanger, Jasmine Garner, Amy Rostad and Jennifer Docherty, I am grateful for all the memorable times we shared together during our adolescence. I treasure our lifelong friendships. To Carolyn Nakade, thank you for making me feel like the smartest person you know. To all my dear friends, near and far, your encouragement and excitement for this book mean the world to me.

To my first fiction writing class, thank you for the conversation that led to the inception of *The Science of Boys*. To the members of the SCBWI Canada West critique groups, thank you for your valuable feedback, especially at the beginning stages. I would also like to thank Sophia Shimada, Hilary Leung, Rebecca Brewer and Jon Kennedy for reading my early versions when I was still experimenting with words. To all the high school students who took the time to talk to me and answer my questions, thank you for offering a unique perspective into your lives. And to my high school readers, saying that the characters were relatable was all I could hope for. A special thanks to Kiran Bassi for your detailed notes.

A big thank you to my editor Kim Aippersbach for knowing just the right questions to ask and for your thoughtful feedback at every stage of the process. I especially enjoyed our in-depth discussions in the presence of tea and pastries. Aidan Parker, intern editor extraordinaire, your stimulating conversations and insight were invaluable. This book wouldn't be the same without you. Thank you to Viktoria Cseh for copyediting and Mary Ann Thompson for proofreading.

Michael Katz, you believed in this project from the start. Thank you for your confidence in me and this idea. To Carol Frank, I am grateful for your vision of this book. And to both of you, I appreciate all that you do behind the scenes. To Elisa Gutiérrez, thank you for your wonderful work on the book design from front to back cover and everything in between. To Gracey Zhang, thank you for giving these characters life on the pages. You are talented beyond belief.

To my parents, I thank you for your support and unconditional love. You have taught me so much, and for that, I am truly grateful. To my husband, thank you for always believing in me and for reminding me to stay active while I wrote. And finally to my children, Ella and Leonardo, you inspire me everyday. My love for you is stronger than all the forces of nature combined.

LIBRARY AND ARCHIVES CANADA CATALOGUING IN PUBLICATION
Title: The science of boys / Emily Seo ; illustrated by Gracey Zhang.
Names: Seo, Emily, author. | Zhang, Gracey, illustrator.
Identifiers: Canadiana (print) 20220166927 | Canadiana (ebook) 20220166935 | ISBN 9781926890401
(hardcover) | ISBN 9781926890371 (softcover) | ISBN 9781990598012 (PDF)
Classification: LCC PS8637.E56 S35 2022 | DDC jC813/.6—dc23

Book design by Elisa Gutiérrez

The text is set in Davis. Titles are set in Brush Up and notes are set in Linger On .

10   9   8   7   6   5   4   3   2   1

Printed and bound in Canada on ancient-forest-friendly paper.

The publisher thanks the Government of Canada, the Canada Council for the Arts and
Livres Canada Books for their financial support. We also thank the Government of the
Province of British Columbia for the financial support we have received through the
Book Publishing Tax Credit program and the British Columbia Arts Council.

EMILY SEO holds a PhD in chemistry from the University of British Columbia and worked in science publishing in Germany. Her experimentation with words resulted in *The Science of Boys*. She currently lives in Vancouver, BC, with her husband and two young scientists.

GRACEY ZHANG is the author and illustrator of the children's book *Lala's Words*, for which she received the Ezra Jack Keats Award. She is also the illustrator of *The Big Bath House*, *Nigel and the Moon* and *The Upside Down Hat*. Born and raised in Vancouver, BC, she is now based in New York City.